"Are you okay?"

Kayla whirled to face the current source of her distress. Preoccupied with jumbled thoughts, she hadn't heard Marcelo enter the store.

She said the first thing that entered her mind. "We're not open yet."

"I've been sick with worry. Where were you?" Marcelo touched her shoulder then his hand slid down her arm and clutched her wrist. "I circled by here twice last night then searched all over town for you."

Kayla studied him carefully. His face, bronzed by the wind and sun, revealed an inherent strength. The shadow of his beard gave him an even manlier aura. His mouth, usually parted in a dazzling display of straight white teeth, was pulled tight by the muscle clenched along his jaw. Worry lined his brow. Something inside her cheered up for a moment. It felt good to have someone care about her. But he still had a few things to answer for.

Books by Jean Kincaid

Love Inspired Heartsong Presents

The Marriage Ultimatum
A Home in His Heart

JEAN KINCAID

and her husband, Dale, are missionaries to the Hispanic people in Old Mexico and the Rio Grande Valley. Her husband pastors Cornerstone Baptist Church in Donna, Texas, where Jean teaches the junior girls' class and sings in the rondalla. They have three adult children and twelve grandchildren. Jean speaks at ladies' retreats and women's events, and enjoys all things mission related. Her favorite time of day is early morning, when she spends time in devotional reading and prayer. Her heart's desire is to create stories that will draw people to a saving knowledge of our Lord Jesus Christ. You may contact her at www.jeankincaid.com.

JEAN KINCAID

A Home in His Heart

HEARTSONG
PRESENTS

Recycling programs
for this product may
not exist in your area.

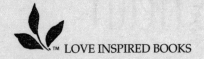

™ LOVE INSPIRED BOOKS

ISBN-13: 978-0-373-48675-5

A HOME IN HIS HEART

Copyright © 2013 by Jean Kincaid

www.LoveInspiredBooks.com

Printed in U.S.A.

Trust in him at all times; ye people. Pour out your heart before him: God is a refuge for us.
—*Psalms* 62:8

This book is dedicated to my mother, Margie Hart Crump, who went to be with the Lord this year. She was the strongest woman I knew and I miss her greatly. Also, to Lucille Dowdy, who bought all my books and handed them out as gifts. She also is now in heaven. My mother wanted me to write her story and Lucille wanted to read my stories. What a great support team I had. I hope to do them proud.

Chapter 1

Marcelo Fuentes followed the trail of dust through the binocular lens, his curiosity piqued by who dared trespass on his land. He urged his horse around a clump of mesquite bushes to get a better look.

"Whoa, boy. Stand still." Raising the binoculars, he focused again, disbelief mingling with surprise at what he saw. A red Mercedes convertible raced along the dirt track. *Idiota!* Who in their right mind would drive that fast along an unused, rutted road in such an expensive car?

The horse blew through its nostrils and stomped, causing him to lose sight of the vehicle. He spurred the horse into a gallop, determined to confront the trespasser and set him straight on a few things. Mainly that he was on private property, and that he should treat his vehicle like a woman—with great care and attention. Not send it barreling down a rutted track.

He arrived just in time to see a suitcase disappear inside the door of his line shack.

"Hey!" he shouted. He almost fell off his horse as the intruder stepped outside.

"Well, 'hey,' yourself."

He closed his mouth with a snap. A beautiful woman, not a man, stared back at him. Hands on her hips, she gave him a big Texas smile, making her honey-brown eyes squint. Her hair, swept back into a catch of some kind, was the color of rich honey.

"I don't suppose you carry a hammer with you?" she asked.

"Beneath the sink. Left side." Marcelo shook his head as if to clear the cobwebs. *What are you thinking, man, to give an intruder—albeit a gorgeous one—directives on where to find your supplies?*

She reappeared seconds later with a sign and prepared to nail it to the outside wall. He slid from the horse and strode to the steps.

"Now, wait just a minute, here." He had to stop this and quick, no matter if she looked like an angel.

"Just a minute, Tex." She tapped the nail a few times till it was secure, then hammered it all the way home. The words read, *As for me and my house, we will serve the Lord.* "That's the only family heirloom I have. It belonged to my grandmother. I only met her a few times, but this was her motto. I figure if it worked for her, it will work for me."

She walked to him and shook his hand, her grip firm.

"I'm Kayla Guerrero. Now, who are you and what are you doing on my land?"

He cast an approving glance over her face. He recognized the plaque. It hung over his neighbor's door until the house flooded a couple years back. By then, his neighbor was in a rest home and passed away two weeks later. He himself had salvaged the little wooden sign after the house had caved, and he'd given the piece to the family attorney. This must be the granddaughter. The lawyer said someone would arrive to claim ownership. He just hadn't said it would be two whole years later.

"Excuse me!" Her voice reclaimed his attention, her smile wavering only slightly. "You are?"

"Wondering if you'd like to sell the property you inherited?" He pointed northeast of where they stood.

"Sell my property? Not on your life!" She spoke as if Marcelo had insulted her.

"You have twenty head of cattle and three horses. That's a lot of work for a woman. Your land has the only natural water source around for miles. I could use that here on my ranch. I'll pay top dollar."

"Not interested. This is family land. I intend to settle here, put down roots. Maybe we could work out a deal with the water. You care for the animals and in return I'll grant you water rights." A sparkle returned to her eyes. She seemed so proud of her suggestion, happy that she'd thought so quickly on her feet.

"Miss, this is the twenty-first century. You don't settle for water rights. You own the water. That's why I'd like to purchase the land. Unless you have loads of money, there is nothing you can do to improve your property, and it's already in a sad state of disrepair."

The woman started to speak several times then held up her hand signaling him to wait. She disappeared into the shack then reappeared, striding forward till they were almost nose to nose.

"Get on your horse and get off my property." She spoke through gritted teeth.

The situation proved too humorous for Marcelo. In spite of himself, he chuckled. "Or what?" he challenged.

She extended her right arm, fingers clutched tightly around a can of mace poised roughly two inches from his eyes.

"Or I'll tell the sheriff there's a blind man staggering around in my yard."

Marcelo figured his mama hadn't raised any fools and his poppi always declared a good run better than a bad stand any day, so he did as the crazy woman asked. He got on his horse and rode off into the sunset. Literally. He squinted against the sun's evening rays and noticed that the cattle he'd fed moments before still munched on the sweet-smelling hay he'd tossed over the fence, uninterested in the tableau before them. She hadn't even thanked him. She probably didn't realize they were her cows.

He turned in the saddle, glancing back at her. She stood defensively, a small pink camouflage canister grasped in one hand, the other raised to shade her eyes. He waved a brief salute; she stiffened and haughtily tossed her head. Marcelo could hold it no longer. Laughter floated up from his throat, rocking his shoulders, deep and jovial. He planned to have the last word with this beautiful spitfire.

He topped the small rise that hid the back of the ranch from Route 281 bypass traffic. He'd chosen the western section of land he and his brothers had inherited. Juan Antonio, the middle son, had chosen the eastern section near the Gulf of Mexico. He'd planted sugar cane. Raoul, the youngest, had been left with the family hacienda, the middle acreage known as the Citrus Queen. Grapefruit, the main crop, along with oranges and lemons, supplied livelihood for fifty-plus workers, and they had squeezed by with a fairly decent crop yield this past winter. Even though the brothers went separate ways with their inheritance, it was understood that the land belonged to the three of them and in time of need, help was guaranteed.

From where he sat astride his horse, he could easily view the spread before him. For miles on the flat land white-faced cattle grazed, their red bodies fat and healthy. A one-story barn that looked more like two small schools, and a grain silo sat off to the right. A mile away he could make out the deep brown terra-cotta roof tiles, complementing the cream-painted stucco walls of the ranch house. He was too far away to make out the arches and the courtyard partially hidden by mesquite trees, palms and tall cactus, but it never failed to move him that God had so blessed and provided. Yes, he had a huge mortgage payment each month, but Lord willing and a few good cattle sales and he would cut the time in half.

But there had been an emptiness in his soul lately

that hadn't been there the past few years as he'd worked long, hard hours to make the ranch a success. Sometimes he'd worked sixteen-hour days with little rest but he'd lived on adrenaline, always celebrating every achievement. Now, even though he still loved and enjoyed his work, he found himself wanting more. Maybe it was seeing Juan Antonio so happy with his fiancée, Carina, and hearing the wedding plans they made. The special looks that passed between them and the loving touches they thought no one noticed. He wasn't sure what caused the restlessness but on days like today it would be nice to share his life with someone.

At the barn entrance, Marcelo removed the saddle and started to brush his horse down.

"*Hola, jefe.* How was the ride?" His foreman, "Flipper" Cantu, took the brush from him and quickly finished the task. Marcelo hired college boys during the summer months to help with roundup, vaccinations, cleanup and mowing. One of the white college boys knew no Spanish and could not pronounce "Felipe," the foreman's name, so he'd called him Flipper. It stuck.

"We've got company."

Flipper looked around quickly. "Where?"

Marcelo brushed the dust from his clothing and walked to the outside faucet to wash his hands. "*Señora* Guerrero's granddaughter moved in this evening."

Flipper gazed at him with a half-bland smile. "What you talking about, boss? Moved in where?"

"The line shack. Lock, stock and barrel. Even hung her gramma's sign on the front porch."

Flipper's smile vanished, wiped away by astonishment. "Now why would she go do a fool thing like that?"

"Not sure, but I intend to find out." Marcelo pulled open the door to his truck. "I'm too tired to worry about it tonight. I'm going to the house." He climbed wearily behind the wheel then as an afterthought said, "Tell the boys not to bother her. I'll feed and care for her livestock until we settle things."

"Sure thing, boss." Flipper pulled the big barn doors closed, jumped on a four-wheeler and headed in the opposite direction.

Kayla stomped into the house, which was more like a hotel room, a war of emotions raging within her. The offensive man had laughed at her. And he'd not stated his name. Could that have been deliberate? She'd wanted to knock him off his high horse. And a beautiful horse it was, at that. The man wasn't too bad to look at, either.

A quick and disturbing thought invaded her emotional rampage. He could have easily been a murderer, could have overpowered her. What if he came back during the night? She had no means of protection. A can of mace wasn't much of a defense. Momentary panic flickered through her. The door had not been locked. She had walked right in. She checked and sure enough, no locks. She began to shake as fearful images built in her mind. She sat down on the bed and fought for control.

The man had not seemed combative or dangerous. He'd been friendly up till the point she demanded he leave. She had not felt threatened. Those were the facts. He'd also been helpful. He told her where the hammer was. How had he known that? He must have worked for her grandmother. Maybe as a handyman. If her grandmother trusted him, then she would, too.

Her courage returned and she looked around for a way to bolt the door.

Her things took up all the available floor space, yet she'd brought only what she'd had in her dorm room. How had her grandmother lived in this small place? Granted, it was larger than the college living quarters; plus she'd roomed with two other girls, so this step up would work nicely. Positive thinking, that's what she needed.

She drove her car around to the back of the house. To her way of thinking, if someone came up the drive and didn't see a vehicle, they'd think no one was home and would leave. Back inside she secured the door with a chair under the doorknob. With the door closed, the only light came from the small bathroom window. She flipped a switch beside the door and light flooded the room. Thank God. The tiny bathroom sink had running water. Another plus. But the closed door had shut off the breeze and in minutes the room was sweltering hot. Toward the top of the back wall, a window air-conditioning unit had been installed. She turned it on high, and cold air filtered slowly over her face. She breathed a sigh of relief. Perfect. This would work, and it was better than some of the places she'd lived in her lifetime.

A small refrigerator occupied one corner of the room; a microwave cart held a collection of ketchup packets, salt and napkins but no microwave. Two chairs and a table made up the kitchenette, but there was neither a stove to cook on nor a kitchen sink. Two doors led off the left, one to the small bathroom, the other to a cubicle the same size as the bathroom. A shovel, various other odd-looking tools, paint cans and a roll of barbed wire sat neatly on the floor or leaned against the inside wall. Why on earth had her grandmother needed those things? Why, still, had she kept them in her house?

She dragged the boxes of clothes, shoes and books into the cubicle room along with the satchel that held her parents' papers, photos and the memorabilia that recorded Kayla's life from birth till now. The cubicle would serve as her closet. She started to unload her toiletries in the bathroom but the shower drain, positioned in the center of the floor, the lack of a stall, shower curtain and cabinet under the sink meant the water from the showerhead most likely would cover every inch of the tiled walls and floor. Surely a man had designed this place. How had her grandmother endured the inconvenience all that time? As soon as she opened her party store, Confetti, and began making a profit, she'd remodel this mess, though she had to admit the tile was beautiful and the sink so clean she'd have no compunction at washing dishes in it.

She sank down on the bed then sneezed. Dust rose in the air around her. She sneezed again. She stood and gently folded the Mexican blanket covering the bed. Digging through one of her boxes, she unearthed sheets and an old lap blanket she'd had since she was a child. She made the bed, took a quick shower in tepid water, then prepared for what she hoped would be the first good night's sleep in two weeks. She glanced at her watch. Nine-thirty. My soul. She hadn't gone to bed this early in years.

As sleep claimed her body, her heart grieved over the great loss she'd recently suffered. Up until last week, she'd ended every day with a call to her parents, talking to one or both of them before she went to sleep. Now there was no one to call. No family members left. She was alone. She felt bereft, set adrift. As exhaustion weighed her down, the sad events of the past week unfolded. She moaned and her legs moved restlessly, fighting an unseen threat. She tried to open her eyes, but her lids refused to cooperate. Like a horror movie, the scenes scrolled unhindered through her mind.

Twin caskets. She stared across them at the grave diggers. Most likely they thought themselves discreetly hidden, and she grieved that they, along with the dour funeral director standing respectfully behind her, were the sole attendees at her beloved parents' burial. They would feel no remorse at lowering the caskets into the hole, tossing in the loose dirt till Mother and Poppy rested in total darkness. She felt a nauseating sense of despair. Alone in the world with no living relatives, her ability to cope weakened. A hot tear rolled down her cheek.

An unusual sight crowded into the dream. She latched on to it, desperate to forget the sadness, straining to leave the events sucking her into the depths of despair. Oh, yes. The man on the horse saluted. Then she heard him laugh. How dare he! A noise lured her from sleep, but she fought to stay under the warm blanket. There it was again. Distressed. Someone in pain, crying out. She sat straight up in bed, her heart pounding. Bawling sounds from what appeared to be animals. Something must be after her cows. She jumped from the bed and grabbed the shovel from the cubicle. Removing the chair from under the doorknob, she stepped out onto the porch. The gray light of dawn had just begun to spread fingers of light over the flat land. Down by the fence, about twenty cows looked curiously back at her, the bawling increasing to decibels guaranteed to gain results if one wanted the noise to cease. She walked slowly toward them, checking left and right for four-legged intruders of a different species. Spying nothing, she reached a hand across the fence, offering comfort through touch. The big animal jerked his head up as if offended.

"What's wrong, fellers?" she cooed. "Did something scare you?" She tried petting another one but jerked her hand back quickly when a wet tongue slapped over her fingers.

"Unless you're offering food, I'd keep my hands on this side of the fence."

Kayla nearly jumped out of her skin. She whirled around to find the man from yesterday striding toward her, carrying a bale of hay. He dropped his bundle at her feet, then cut the string holding it together. Quickly he threw sections of hay across the fence in different spots. The cattle crowded around each other and the noise ceased.

"So they were hungry." How simpleminded of her not to know. Embarrassed, she looked away.

"Yep. Five-thirty every morning they make their way here expecting to be fed. Inconsiderate beasts, right?"

Kayla looked up into dark eyes brimming with merriment. Her sense of humor took over and she laughed in answer. "Is it really just five-thirty?"

"Yes, ma'am. In about ten minutes the sun will pop up over the horizon and by lunchtime it will be hot enough to fry an egg on cement."

"Now that was corny." Kayla watched the side of his mouth tilt upward in a saucy grin. He stood tall and straight like a towering spruce. The light-colored T-shirt displayed his muscular arms. The outline of his shoulders strained against the fabric and the dark shadow of his beard gave him an even manlier aura. Suddenly she realized he studied her in much the same way, and she cringed inwardly at what he must see. She turned on her heel and hurried to the house, not stopping to explain.

She climbed into the center of the bed, listening as the truck cranked up and drove away. She hugged her knees to her. She could still see his eyebrow quirked questioningly. He'd caught her staring, checking him out. She groaned and flopped back against the pillows. She wondered for just a brief moment why it bothered her so much that he'd seen her with her hair all mussed up, no makeup on and wearing a college T-shirt and Pilates pants. Why couldn't she have had on something alluring, her makeup on and her hair sleek? She felt certain the cattle would have appreciated the effort.

Chapter 2

Dressed, organized and in her right mind, Kayla searched the place for food. Above and below the pint-size, eye-level refrigerator were cabinets, the bottom one filled with paper towels, toilet paper and a few bath towels. In the upper cabinet, more ketchup packets, a can of Vienna sausages and a jar of peanut butter were all she could find. A trip to the grocery store couldn't be avoided, yet she hadn't planned on it today. She had more important things to do, things involving her new business. There was no time to make a list of all the things she would need before she went to town. She excelled in to-do lists and schedules. "A structure fanatic," her dad often called her.

She heard a vehicle approaching from the back property. On the porch she watched the man from this morning step down from his truck, maneuvering a Whataburger bag and a steaming large coffee.

"What's this?" She could not explain how ridiculously happy she was to see him again. She noticed the clean-shaven jaw and change of clothes and caught a whiff of cologne.

"Breakfast."

"What if I don't eat breakfast?" He stopped midstride, his surprise obviously genuine, and she regretted the gibe. He instantly recognized her comment for the jest it was and turned back to his truck, a teasing glint in his eyes.

"I'll just take this back with me."

"Wait." She tentatively motioned him to the steps. "I'm starving. Thank you for thinking of me."

"Not a problem. Figured you haven't had time to buy groceries." He handed over the food but acknowledged her invitation to sit with a slight shake of his head. "Gotta run. Have an early appointment."

Surprise held her immobile a few seconds. He'd gone out of his way to bring her breakfast. How she'd love to take a few moments and analyze the gesture, but he already had the truck door open. "Well, thanks again. You're a real lifesaver."

He gave a curt nod of farewell and that same half salute that had tormented her dreams, a slight tip of two fingers to the edge of his hat.

Kayla ate the sausage biscuit, saving the top piece of bread for the strawberry jam packet she found in the bottom of the bag. She drank the coffee and went over last-minute preparations for leasing a building for Confetti. Excitement rose and with a pulse-pounding certainty she knew exciting things would happen that day.

Three hours later and Kayla was the proud owner of a five-year lease on a six-thousand-square-foot building, complete with storage room and loading dock. A little more space than she bargained for but if she went forward with future plans, she could expand from just party supplies to include catering. She stood outside and gazed up at the curved gables and Spanish baroque-style architecture that copied that of the Alamo. Her heart sang with delight.

"You're staring at that place like a kid in a candy store."

Kayla jumped at the sound of the voice, her swift gaze taking in the woman before her and the car she'd just exited. Lost in daydreams she hadn't even heard the car approach.

"Better than candy," she agreed. "Better, even, than breakfast this morning from the cowboy."

"Now that sounds intriguing." Sweat beaded the young woman's upper lip, and she fanned her face with some papers she held in her hand.

Kayla pointed to the store, a silent invitation for the woman to join her. "Would you happen to be Alma Cantu?"

"The one and only." She huffed as if the short walk had worn her out. Kayla wondered at Alma's obvious lack of stamina.

"Alfredo said you were looking for an office manager."

They entered the cool interior. Alfredo Soto, the

agent who leased the building, had mentioned he knew someone perfect for the job, but Kayla needed someone active.

"Yes, he called fifteen minutes ago, and I've raced like a Nascar driver to get here. *Perdoname.* I work on the south end of town near the border. I literally ran through the parking lot to get to my car then barely missed several red lights. I did not want to miss this interview."

Well, that explained the shortness of breath.

"I'm sorry there's no place to sit. If you'd like, I'll treat you to lunch and we can discuss what the job requires."

Thirty minutes into their meal, Kayla knew she'd found a gem. From Alma's previous job in retail, she'd built an extensive list of party-supply contacts from Laredo, San Antonio and Corpus Christi. What a blessing. This would cut down on the amount of time it would take to set up new accounts.

"Do you have an order sheet ready?"

Kayla laughed out loud. "I've had a wish list since tenth grade." She opened her organizer and extracted a sheaf of papers that looked more like a contract. "I've grouped it into categories so nothing will be left out."

Alma perused the list, her eyes darting from one side to the other. "You know," Alma spoke matter-of-factly, "you should go with us next month to The Christmas House in Falfurrias." She nodded several times, then looked up. "They have a huge sale in July and clean out their warehouse. You could stock up on all kinds of Christmas decorations for that season, and we could decorate for any parties we cater. They might share their local suppliers list and that would be a huge plus."

"Who's going and would they mind me tagging along?"

"Of course they wouldn't mind. There are about nine of us. We take the church van and make a day of it. Let's see." She put a finger out and clicked off the numbers. "Carina Garza just got engaged and plans to have a Christmas wedding. She hopes to find unusual things to use at the reception. Adele Rivas from The Citrus Queen goes every year. They're the only two our age. Pastor's wife, Kim, and her friend DeAnn and then a couple of senior citizens finish out the group. You would certainly be welcome."

Alma's easy acceptance of Kayla touched her heart. She'd never had many close friends but she felt positive Alma would be someone important in her life.

She noted the date in her organizer and accepted the check for their meal.

"When can you start work?" She felt her eyes widen as Alma laughed infectiously.

"I gave my notice two weeks ago after praying and trusting that God was guiding my decision. Alfredo told me you will be closed on Sundays and at six in the evening, which was what I had prayed for. Being more involved in church has become first priority for me." Kayla saw the sheen of purpose in the other woman's eyes. "I've asked the Lord to send me a Christian mate who is full-time in Christian ministry, but so far he's said 'no.'"

Kayla was too startled by Alma's statement to offer a comment. Apparently none was needed as she continued.

"And I understood perfectly. Why would the good Lord give me a husband who wanted to serve in the church if I couldn't even attend with him?" Alma paused for breath and pushed back a wayward strand of hair as they settled into Kayla's Mercedes convertible. "So, to answer your question, tomorrow is my last day at my current job, and I'm available Monday."

"Then you're hired. Hours are from nine to six Monday through Friday and an occasional Saturday." She quoted a salary figure that Alma agreed to, and they arrived back at Confetti in high spirits.

Kayla spent the rest of the day getting extra keys made, having the electricity account changed to her name and billing address, setting up a commercial checking account at the local bank and hiring a man to build a U-shaped counter for the store. She sat on the floor with her laptop and placed Confetti's first order. The amount wiped out her personal checking account, and she'd have to wait three days—bank's requirements not hers—before ordering from Confetti's new checking account. Excitement raced through her veins. She grabbed her phone to call and share her day with Poppy and Mother. Wait. Her parents were gone. She had no one to tell. A raw and primitive grief overwhelmed her. Bereft and desolate, she jumped up and found her to-do list. Staying busy would help.

She drove to the local Wally World and bought a hot plate with two heating units, a small frying pan and pot, several kitchen utensils and food items. Dusk settled over the flat land of the Rio Grande as she turned onto the road to her house. She crested the little knoll surrounding the stagnant pond that boasted her natural water supply, and caught a brief glimpse of red taillights disappearing down the dirt track behind her house. Cattle munched happily on hay tossed across the fence.

So the unnamed stranger had been a good neighbor again this evening. On impulse she decided to follow him. She'd simply thank him and let him know that from now on she'd feed her animals herself. She'd have to figure out *how* to feed them and how to get hay here without a truck, but look it up on Google she would.

Five minutes into the drive the convertible bumped and jolted over ruts and sagebrush. His truck would have no difficulty navigating this route but her beautiful new car suffered much. Fifteen minutes later she flipped her headlights on and strained to make out the track. Finally she spotted lights to a homestead and breathed a sigh of relief. The big truck sat near a building—a barn perhaps, yet not the usual second-story type with a loft. A man exited the building but it wasn't her handsome stranger.

"Can I help you, ma'am?"

Kayla was glad that the semidarkness hid the flush in her cheeks. How did you ask to speak to someone when you didn't know his name? "The guy that drives that truck. Does he live here?"

"You mean *patrón? Sí,* he is here. I will get him for you."

So the man had a legitimate job. Her eyes kept drift-

ing to the house on her left. It boasted stunning architecture and fabulous landscaping, to say the least.
Cacti stood as tall as the house; beautiful palm trees
lined the entryway to the courtyard. Peaceful came to
mind—as well as wealthy. Then her breath caught in
her throat as Zorro walked toward her. Well, not Zorro
exactly, but the handsome breakfast-delivery man who
fed her cattle.

"Kayla, what's up?" The way he said her name caused
a little flutter in the top of her stomach. "And please tell
me you didn't drive that car through the field."

Kayla, for reasons she couldn't fathom, found herself
tongue-tied. She studied his face outlined by shadows. It
was so easy to get lost in the way he stared back at her.

His expression stilled and grew serious. "What is
it, Kayla?"

Helpless to halt her embarrassment at following him,
Kayla tried to find the words to explain. "I'm tired, it's
dark and I acted on impulse."

Smiling, he leaned forward and opened her door. She
met the smile and the hand that was offered.

She exited the car and noticed he held her hand a bit
longer than necessary.

"This is awkward." Nervously she ran a hand through
her hair. "Um…"

He held up a hand to silence her. "Things should
never be awkward between friends and neighbors, so
why don't we start with what brought you here and
how I can help."

"I saw the cattle eating and wanted to thank you for
feeding them again. I followed your taillights, though

I didn't know the road is just a dirt track, not even as wide as the entry road. I wondered where you lived and curiosity got the best of me, I guess. On top of all that I don't even know your name."

She leaned back against the car and waited. The lights from the house behind him shone in her eyes and she could only make out his outline. She was unable to see the expression on his face or the look in his eyes, which she found very unsatisfactory.

"That's a problem easily solved." He motioned her to precede him up the walk, explaining as they approached the house. "My name is Marcelo Fuentes. My friends call me Marc. This is my home—" he leaned forward and opened a huge wooden door that couldn't have been less than ten feet tall "—and you're welcome." She looked up and caught the gleam in his eyes. "For feeding the animals and to my home. Welcome, that is."

Kayla turned and a soft gasp escaped her. Cool terra-cotta tile glistened in the entryway and the sitting area beckoned her farther into the house. Tall columns spaced eight feet apart hugged a huge circular room with a skylight through which the moon cast a soft glow over the furniture. At a flick of his hand light invaded the coziness. From where she stood, Kayla could see into part of the dining room. Her tiny house would fit into any one of these rooms. More than once. This house oozed wealth and exquisite taste, and Kayla suddenly felt uncomfortable. The man fed her cattle. She'd followed him like an amateur private investigator. Oh, law…she swallowed a groan…she'd threatened him with mace.

* * *

Marcelo noticed her expressive face change and said, "You don't like my house?"

He watched the corner of her mouth tip up. "Are you kidding? This place is gorgeous."

"Then why the sudden look of horror?" His question seemed to amuse her, then she shook her head.

She turned teasing eyes upon him. "Some things are better left unsaid, so I'm not telling you. Now please tell me there's a fully equipped kitchen behind that wall." She took a step forward. "May I?"

"Sure, but um—" he pointed down a hallway "—that direction."

"Really?" She walked to the dining room. "But the dining room is here. Wouldn't that put the kitchen too far away?"

"Come see."

Together they walked down the wide hall with several closed double doors. A breakfast nook could be seen at the end. As they turned the corner Marcelo felt deep gratification at her resonant "wow." A curved kitchen wasn't usually what one expected. At the far end, an arched opening led directly into the formal dining room. The kitchen itself was spacious with a plethora of gadgets, some Marcelo himself knew nothing about. Adele, from the family homestead The Citrus Queen, had outfitted the kitchen when the finishing touches were required.

Marcelo laughed when Kayla opened one of the cabinets that just happened to hide the refrigerator. "Are you hungry?"

Kayla quickly closed the door. "I'm so sorry. Curiosity got the best of me. The refrigerator door looks exactly like the cabinets." Stains of scarlet appeared on her cheeks, and she walked back to the hallway in a hurry he just knew meant she was about to leave. He couldn't let that happen. For some reason unbeknownst to him, he wanted to spend more time with her.

"My bad. Here." He took her elbow and gently turned her back to the kitchen. "I didn't ask if you were hungry because you looked in my refrigerator. I asked because I'd like you to stay and have dinner with me. I planned to throw a few steaks on the grill and with your help we'll have veggies, too. That'll be a real treat for me since I usually just have meat." He hoped his pitiful request for help would sway her.

"You usually eat only meat?" Her voice held a trace of laughter and incredulity.

Hastily he drew her to the island that occupied the center of the room. He set a bowl in front of her and pulled the makings of a salad from the fridge. He had no time to examine his suddenly buoyant mood. "Yeah, I'm afraid so. Adele washes the veggies and puts them in plastic bags but that means I have six or seven little bags to open, then close, then put back in the fridge. That's a lot of hoopla when I'm hungry and in a hurry." He grabbed the marinating steaks and checked the date on a loaf of bread. "Much easier to grill meat, grab a tortilla and the A.1. sauce."

He set the steaks on the counter and as casually as he could manage asked, "So how do you like yours?"

She hesitated a moment then, "Oh, my steak. Well done, please."

At the French doors he turned on the terrace lights, illuminating the patio and grill. In minutes he had things going and went back inside for a spray bottle of water. He might cook occasionally for himself, but that didn't mean he'd mastered it. That an occasionally charred steak was more the norm made him overly cautious not to mess tonight's meal up.

They sat down to a perfect grilled steak and a crunchy salad. Kayla had buttered bread and found the garlic salt, and seeing no dressing in the fridge, had made her own. For some reason that pleased him, and his reaction to it seemed to amuse her. "It's just salad dressing, Marcelo, not rocket science."

"But it's very unusual to find a woman nowadays that knows her way around the kitchen, much less how to make something from scratch."

"You had all the ingredients. I just mixed them up. And it really depends on what kind of women you normally hang around with." A glint of humor flickered in the eyes that met his. "There are lots of us out there. We're listed under gifted and talented. In this case, gifted and talented in this case goes with a master's degree."

Something warm and enchanting relaxed his shoulders and he continued the gentle sparring. "So you graduated from cake-decorating class?"

Green eyes flashed a warning but her lips trembled with the need to smile. "Yes. And Food Preparation 101. All with honors."

He lifted his hand and rested his fingers over hers for a brief second. "I'm joking, of course. What's your master's degree in?"

"Business management. And I minored in home economics."

He'd been had. Her wide-eyed innocence was merely a smoke screen for an independence of spirit and the ability to laugh at herself and tease others. Beautiful eyes that brightened with merriment or blazed with icy contempt. He liked that. He liked her. The future suddenly looked bright. He might like having a neighbor, even if she was a squatter in his own line shack.

"And what type of business would you like to manage?"

"My own. I'm opening a party-supply business named Confetti on Eighteenth Street in McAllen. I signed the lease today."

He could see the excitement in her eyes and it mirrored the feelings he'd had when he inherited the ranch. "Are you a driven person?" To his delight she got his meaning again.

"When it comes to Confetti, yes. It's been a childhood dream and every step along the way motivates me even more, feeding my desire to see it to fruition." She took a sip of tea. "Does that make sense?"

"Oh, yes. That's how it was when I inherited this ranch. I worked sixteen-hour days but never seemed tired, yet I had to be exhausted. Even the obstacles weren't that aggravating because I knew they were teaching me how to manage this place."

Marcelo found it easy talking to her because she

seemed to hang on to his every word and she understood. It felt good.

"Right. That's how it was when I had to change my location from New York to here. It seemed like a big difference, for sure, but it was really just the same design and intent for business with a few minor adjustments. And now every moment I spend away from those plans seems like wasted time and I can't wait to see the walls hanging full of balloons and themed party supplies." Her eyes were alight with the excitement she felt and Marcelo thought he'd never seen a more beautiful, animated woman in his life. His smile broadened in approval.

Chapter 3

Kayla signed the paper on the UPS driver's clipboard, then looked in wonder at the boxed inventory she and Alma would have to organize and hang on the numerous wall-to-ceiling metal pegs.

"Oh, this is so exciting." Alma's eyes gleamed with a sheen of purpose. "Can we start opening boxes or are they numbered in order? Do you have a diagram of where everything goes?"

Kayla chuckled. "No diagram. Let's look at the order forms to verify what we've bought and check that it's all here, then we'll decide which wall gets the girl stuff and do the opposite wall in boys." Kayla ran her hand over the tops of several boxes. There was barely room to walk between them. Some were stacked higher than her head. This was going to take time, but they had roughly three weeks before the grand opening so it shouldn't be a problem.

It took a little over three hours to open each box, count the contents, check them off and arrange them in the order everything would be displayed. They laughed, ooh and ahh'd over each party pack they opened and finally began to place them on the walls. Kayla took the girl side and had a hard time deciding which she liked better amongst princesses, explorers, kittens and rainbows. An array of colors soon lined both walls; party packs with bags, napkins, plates, cups, favors, even confetti and cards. Lunchtime came and went and when they finally felt hunger pangs it was close to quitting time. Neither of them wanted to leave so they ordered pizza and continued working till every theme that had been ordered was represented either on the wall or on the chest-high shelves in between. The unused inventory they stashed in the back storage room for later.

At a little past seven Kayla locked the door and headed wearily for home. When she pulled up in front of the house her neighbor sat in the lone rocker on her porch, his feet crossed and propped on the rail. A flicker of apprehension coursed through her. She didn't really know him and even though they'd shared a meal together and he kindly fed her cattle, she still felt disturbing quakes in her serenity when he was near. It vexed her somewhat that she seemed to be more afraid of her reaction to him than any fear of him.

"Howdy, neighbor." His slow drawl with a Spanish inflection made her chuckle.

"You'd never be mistaken for a cowboy with that accent." She sank down on the swing facing him.

"You wound me deeply. I've worked hard and long to lose my accent." He let his feet drop to the floor with a thud.

"Really?"

"Yes, really." Amusement flickered in the eyes that met hers. "When I was a kid, our church had a bus route, and they would go to the colonials and pick up children and bring them to church. I told my teacher I didn't want to come to church anymore, that I was tired of all the Mexicans."

"Oh, no, you didn't." Kayla couldn't help laughing aloud. "What did she say?"

"She told me to look in a mirror, that I *was* a Mexican. I ran from the room crying, looking for my mom."

"And?" Kayla prompted.

"Mom gently broke the sad news. 'Yep, you're a Mexican, sonny boy. Get used to it.'"

"That's hysterical." Kayla couldn't control her burst of laughter.

"So I'm thinking the accent sounds a little like Speedy Gonzales and I'm good with that."

A comfortable silence settled around them. Kayla became lost in the moment, reviewing the events of the day in her mind. She and Alma had accomplished so much, but they were far from ready to open the store. The computer system would need to be set up, and vendor accounts added with addresses and contact numbers. But it was so much fun she hated to think of the crash that would eventually come from fatigue and burnout. She needed to pace herself and take care that Alma did not overdo it, either.

"Penny for them."

She reined her thoughts back to the present. "I was thinking about all we accomplished today at Confetti."

"Good day?"

"Perfect day. We unpacked inventory and checked lists. That's always fun. There's still a lot to do, though." Even though he gazed steadily at her, she couldn't tell if he were truly interested or not, so she changed the subject. "And how was your day?"

"Not so perfect. The fence was down in an area near the 77 Expressway and some cattle decided to cross the road to greener pasture. We spent the day rounding them up and repairing the fence."

"Hard work?"

"Hot work." He stood and pulled something from his pocket. He handed it to her.

"What's this for?" She stared at the keys he'd placed in her hand.

"I put a lock on your door and a chain lock, too."

She stood up, surprised and immensely pleased. "That was a nice thing to do. Thank you so much." Without thinking, she gave him a brief hug. She stepped out of his encircling arms barely smothering a groan. Must she be so spontaneous?

"You're welcome." His voice sounded gruff. He stepped off the porch and all but ran to his truck. "Good night. See you tomorrow," he called over his shoulder.

She stood alone, uncertainty twisting her insides. Finally she admitted to herself that it bothered her that he might think she was too forward. That could only mean that she cared. She sat back down on the swing and hugged her knees to her. The sun had set over the horizon but there was still light enough to see her surroundings. The cattle had moved off closer to the water and a light breeze cooled the stifling heat of the day. She had plans, dreams and high hopes. She would not put a damper on that by worrying about what a guy thought of her. Even if he did make her feel funny things inside.

Marcelo arrived home and had no memory of the journey getting there. Kayla had smelled like the bougainvillea flower in full bloom. Fruity and smooth. Her face had been soft and her hair brushed his cheek. And he'd lost his ability to speak. Then like a fool he'd rushed to his truck as if repelled by her touch. She must think him a total imbecile.

But she appeared so happy and grateful for the small favor he'd done her, which was nothing time consuming. Apparently she'd been uncomfortable with the door having no lock. He should have thought of it sooner. There were a few other things that needed fixing and would make her life a bit easier. He'd see about those things tomorrow and if the Lord saw fit to bless him with another hug from the beautiful Kayla, then he'd consider that payment in full.

He picked up his Bible from the nightstand beside the bed and leaned against the headboard to read. He'd skipped a few days, and he needed to get back on track. He knew without daily reading, prayer and meditating on the things of God, his plans and dreams had no chance of coming to fruition. He'd tried it on his own and didn't like the outcome of wasted time and resources. He may have to wait sometimes to get exactly what was right for his life but he'd found it was better to follow God's plans than his own.

He read Proverbs 18:22, which said, "Whoso findeth a wife findeth a good thing and obtaineth favor of the Lord." He closed the Bible and slid down the bed, placed his hands behind his head and sought sleep. He wouldn't mind finding a wife. He was tired of being alone. In the short time he'd known Kayla, she'd pierced the dark loneliness that had become his constant companion. She invaded his thoughts all during the day and now the quick hug and softness of her skin would most likely torment him till he could see her again and prove whether it was real or just a figment of his imagination.

Yep. Finding a wife was next on his agenda. But she'd have to be a Christian and love the Lord. She needed to love ranching, too, because that was his life and it was non-negotiable. If they were divided over that minor detail like he and Larisa had been, then the relationship was doomed from the start. He liked spontaneous, too. Spontaneous hugs, spontaneous kisses; yes, that would have to be a requirement in a wife of his.

His last thought as sleep claimed his body was how happy Kayla would be tomorrow when she arrived home. Spontaneity was a good thing.

"Mmm, decadent." Kayla licked the chocolate off the tip of her finger.

"Yeah, tantalizing." Alma added a few more hot drops of the mixture onto wax paper.

"A gift for the emotions." Josh, Alma's eighteen-year-old nephew added with a grin.

"Definitely engages the senses," Alma agreed.

Kayla chuckled. She loved the excitement of discovering something new. That her coworkers shared that excitement with her made it even better. "We have to stop eating the profits. Come over here, Josh, and swing this paddle. Alma, go make something beautiful."

Kayla relinquished the huge wooden paddle to her newest part-time employee, rolling her eyes but unable to stop the huge grin, enjoying the camaraderie with the people she was bossing around. She'd hired Josh this morning and had interviews this evening with more part-time applicants.

"You got it, boss." Alma saluted. "I came back to see if we would actually have a batch of Confetti drops ready to be packaged—then you had to go and pour such scrumptious stuff out here to tempt us. Now you're running me out. Never knew you were so mean and hurtful." Alma ran a finger over the stirring spoon, then licked the creamy froth with a loud smacking noise. "Mean and hurtful, that's what I say."

"Yeah? Well, you'll thank me when those extra pounds *don't* show up on your hips." Kayla pointed to a tray of foil-covered drops of chocolate. They didn't resemble "kisses" but were unique in their own design. The machine had arrived yesterday and they'd put it together earlier this morning and this was their trial batch of chocolate candy. Kayla had created their own design and hoped this would enhance their sales and become one of their main centerpieces at weddings, showers, Valentine banquets and other special occasions. She wanted it up and running before their grand opening. Her plan was for Confetti to have several signature items that defined the difference between it and other party-planning businesses.

Kayla closed the manila folder. She wrote "W2 forms" at the top of it, inserted the slip of paper into the plastic holder, and hung the file in the cabinet. Hiring new employees meant more paperwork, and she found she liked the business part of Confetti as much as she liked the creative part.

She looked around the room she'd chosen as an office. A little paint would cover the spot where a huge mural depicting the battle of the Alamo covered the wall. With a couple of shelves added, she could store completed decorative projects.

She yawned and stretched. She'd worked into the wee hours last night stocking inventory and placing items strategically to catch the buyer's eye. She'd run on adrenaline, but now felt drained. Sleep tempted her to lay her head on the desk for a few seconds. She resisted. If she slept now, tonight all the fears and uncertainties about starting a new business and being on her own would return and plague her, robbing her of much-needed rest. Better to fall into bed too exhausted to think. She stood and walked into the main area of the store.

She was so satisfied with what she saw. The room now consisted of wall-to-wall shelves and a comfortable sitting area for people to rest while their friends or spouses shopped.

During the weeks they'd worked together, Alma had explained that she wanted to design centerpieces for parties of all types and then change the packaging each month so that satisfied customers would return often. And Kayla quickly learned that Alma could make centerpieces that rivaled those in several of the chain craft stores. In fact, no one in New York made prettier gift baskets than Alma—at least not that Kayla had seen, and she had frequented many places while gathering ideas and making plans for her own store. Now Alma would also design centerpieces as well as baskets that included their own signature chocolates. This added a dimension to Confetti that Kayla had only dreamed of, and it had come together without an ounce of help from her. She felt so blessed. The Lord surely smiled upon her. She needed to get in church and give her all to Him because He'd certainly been good to her.

Kayla turned to watch Josh's progress in cooling the thick chocolate mixture he poured out on the marble slab. The wooden paddle he worked back and forth was about half the size of a boat oar. He dipped and turned the chocolate then dragged the paddle through, the scent sweet and tantalizing.

She studied the recipe hanging from a clip on the cabinet door. She put cream on to heat, then chopped a block of chocolate. The cream boiled and she carefully poured it over the chocolate. When it cooled, she would put on gloves and roll the congealed mixture into small balls to insert into one of what she hoped to be her best-selling items: Truffles de Confetti.

"When people taste these you're gonna have to make

more than one batch a week." Josh scooped the cooled chocolate into what resembled a stainless-steel dustpan then poured it into the melter that held more hot chocolate. According to the instructions, stirring the cold and hot together would diminish air bubbles and the concoction would set up perfectly.

"Well, we will cross that bridge when we come to it." Kayla glanced at the clock on the new stove. "I just want to offer something different, and hopefully this will snag customers' attention at our grand opening." She set the timer and breathed a sigh of relief. So far so good.

Nervous butterflies fluttered in her stomach. Finally she'd been granted the opportunity to realize her dreams, and everything was fitting together perfectly. Carpenters had worked yesterday to finish the small kitchen layout in the huge back part of the building that was mostly used for inventory. If sales were good, she hoped to expand the kitchen to offer catering as well as supplies. Last week Kayla had received her packet for the catering license, and she had followed the instructions explicitly. She was to meet with a board of food inspectors to discuss why and how her business would include fresh-food items and benefit the town, which already lacked for nothing.

"Josh, I'll help you put that into the molds and you can finish the truffles, okay?"

"Sure thing." Together they lifted the pot and poured the liquid into an unusual-looking contraption that when turned on dispensed equal amounts into molds. It was a miniature machine and would only dispense a dozen at a time but with several batches, they would achieve all that they needed. At least she hoped so. If they arrived at the place where they needed more than a few batches a week, she'd purchase a commercial machine to do the job.

Later that evening, she hired two girls to work in the evenings and on weekends. Sara and Heidi were the same age and she hoped they turned out to be reliable employees. She also hoped the sure-of-himself, handsome Josh would not give her problems with the girls but she'd worry about that later. For now, her little family had grown to the five of them and she loved it.

Thinking of family, her mind went to Marcelo Fuentes. She hadn't seen him in over a week. Funny how her mind wandered to thoughts of him several times a day, yet she'd known him such a brief time. Was he avoiding her? Maybe he thought she was chasing him, that she'd been too forward.

Marcelo entered his house hot, dusty and tired to the bone. His day had been a total disaster from start to finish. A sprinkler head in his irrigation system had broken and they still didn't have it rotating correctly. He was one of the few ranchers in Texas that grass fed his cattle, only occasionally offering grain to make the meat a bit more tender. The state agricultural department delivered water into a canal that ran through his property in different places. He had several movable water-sprinkler systems connected to these canals that kept the grass growing and provided feed for his cattle. They would have to start on it again early in the morning and hopefully repair it before the sun delivered its hottest rays.

Frustration gnawed at him because he had not accomplished the things he'd planned for Kayla. He'd neither seen nor heard from her lately, and he felt an inexplicable feeling of emptiness. His mind refused to recognize the significance of that. He was simply responding to a person in need—and she was one needy female. He loved the way her honey-brown hair felt against his cheek and the way her eyes most often regarded him with amusement. Their friendly bantering relaxed him.

Weariness enveloped him as he stepped into the shower, his muscles screaming from the strain of reaching above his head for hours on end. His back ached between his shoulder blades. A man could grow old really fast working like he had today. Only one person could make him feel human again and he knew with certainty he would get back in his truck and drive to Kayla's. He wanted to see her; he needed to see her, and even though he'd already fed her cattle he'd find some excuse.

As he dressed he became aware of a delicious smell wafting through the bedroom door. Flipper must have brought him supper. They'd both been dog tired and Flip could hardly wait to get home to his wife's cooking. Every so often they shared with him, and today it would be much appreciated.

He strolled into the kitchen, his shirt unbuttoned, his hair towel-dried and mussed. And there before him stood the occupier of his thoughts. She removed something from the oven that smelled absolutely divine then turned to face him. Her eyes dropped from his face to his chest and then a blush like a shadow ran over her cheeks. He felt the tense lines on his face start to relax. When her eyes swept over him again he almost laughed out loud. He buttoned his shirt.

"I hope you don't mind." She pointed to the food. "I found this recipe pinned to one of my boards online and wanted to try it out. I don't have an oven and your foreman said to come on in, that it would be okay as long as I didn't set the house on fire. So—" she slid what looked like a bread ring onto a plate "—wanna share?"

Gesturing with a sweeping motion, he invited her to sit. He poured them glasses of tea and gathered two forks and some napkins. They sat at the center island and he quickly blessed the food. They ate from the same plate. Some type of bread roll filled with chunks of chicken, spices and vegetables.

"This is fantastic." He spoke with his mouth full and she smacked him playfully on the arm.

"Don't talk with your mouth full."

"What's this called?" He never cooked other than the grill, and this was a real treat.

"A chicken and broccoli ring." She ate dainty little bites and he paused to watch. He'd been shoveling it in and half his side of the ring was almost gone compared to a third of hers. "It's so simple to fix. The filling ingredients are chicken, chopped broccoli, cream of chicken soup, mayonnaise and a few spices. The outside is made from crescent rolls." She looked up then, a teasing glint in her eyes. "But that's not really why I came."

"No?" He liked the camaraderie between them. It crossed his mind briefly that just moments before, his body had been engulfed in tides of weariness and exhaustion. Now here he sat, rejuvenated and with a huge feeling of satisfaction.

She hopped down from the bar stool and picked up a package of foil lying near her purse. She slipped back into her seat and turned toward him, her knee brushing against his. "Close your eyes." She began to unwrap the foil.

"Should I be afraid?" he teased.

"You should always be afraid when a woman tells you to close your eyes." She paused in the unwrapping and directed a meaningful look at him. He obediently closed his eyes. He heard the foil rustle. "Now open your mouth."

He smelled the chocolate before it ever touched his lips, but when he tasted it, he couldn't stop his reaction. "Mmm, now that's good stuff."

"You really like it?"

He opened his eyes and caught the hopeful, expectant look on her face. "I think that's the best chocolate I've ever tasted. What is it?" He broke off another bite and popped it in his mouth.

"It's a family recipe. My dad used to make this from scratch. I want to include it in the catering end of Confetti and use it for special occasions only, so that it can become a major money maker for the business." She placed a small piece in her mouth and he fought the urge to lean forward and kiss her. He had no intentions, though, of scaring her away or rushing things. He thoroughly enjoyed the friendship they shared right now.

"I think that's a great idea." He pushed back their plates then shifted to place both arms on the edge of the island countertop. "You're really serious about this store of yours. You're confident you can make a success of it?"

Her brow furrowed and her lips parted in surprise. "Why would you ask me that? You don't think I can do it?"

"No. No," he exclaimed. "I was just thinking about all the good cooks we have in the Rio Grande Valley and was wondering if the competition is tough."

"Well, we won't be doing ordinary cuisine. Ours will be prix fixe and exquisite fare."

"What's that?"

"A set menu at a fixed or set price but with unusual and tasteful food."

Marcelo watched her expression still and grow serious. "What are you thinking?"

"I need to get in church. Each time I think of being a success, I think of what one of my professors in college said. He said the way to guarantee success in any part of our lives is to first make sure it's God's will, and second to give our business back to the Lord and do our best to live and please Him."

"Sounds like good advice." Marcelo could not help the happiness soaring through him. But he needed to know one more thing. "Are you a Christian?"

"Yes, I accepted the Lord when I was eleven but I still don't know what it all means. I've never gone to church regularly. I just know that He has guided me and protected me. Does that make sense?"

There was a pensive shimmer in her beautiful eyes. Marcelo longed to take her in his arms and comfort her, to explain about the Lord, to make her comfortable in her walk with the Creator. "Makes perfect sense. He moves into our hearts for eternity and He does exactly what you said. He guides and protects. I have an idea." Marcelo had an indefinable feeling of rightness when she looked at him with pure trust and a slight shake of her head. She agreed even before he voiced his suggestion. "Come to church with me Sunday. It will be the perfect day to start a new habit—regular church attendance."

Chapter 4

Let him kiss me with the kisses of his mouth: for
thy love is better than wine.
Because of the savour of thy good ointments thy
name is as ointment poured forth, therefore do
the virgins love thee. Draw me, we will run after
thee: the king hath brought me into his
chambers: we will be glad and rejoice in thee,
we will remember thy love more than wine: the
upright love thee.

Kayla felt an unwelcome blush cover her cheeks.
Standing beside Marcelo, listening to the pastor read
the Scripture passage, she wondered briefly just what
kind of message this would be. When the reading ended,
they sat so close together he had to place his arm on the

back of the bench. The church was packed and a family of seven occupied the rest of the pew.

Marcelo's fragrant, balmy cologne tantalized her, and at first Kayla had a hard time concentrating on the pastor's words. However, the more he spoke on the intimate relationship between Jesus the bridegroom and the church as the bride, the more engrossed she became. She'd never heard anything like it and a desire to experience that closeness with the Lord prompted her to go forward to pray during the invitational song. She felt happiness swell till her heart was full and could hardly wait to read her Bible. The pastor had explained that prayer and daily Bible reading helped gain that intimacy that the inner man craved. Such a feeling of peace overcame her and tears filled her eyes. She wished she'd known this earlier in her life. How she would have enjoyed the fellowship of a God who truly cared.

After church Marcelo took her to a local hole-in-the-wall restaurant where she ate the best fajitas ever made, with rice and Charro beans, her favorite. The waitresses and even the owner came and sat at their table for brief moments, all of them teasing and with obvious curiosity as to who she was.

"So you bring all your girlfriends here, do you?" Kayla decided she could do a bit of teasing herself. At the inquiring lift of his left eyebrow, she explained. "They all seem very interested in who I am so I'm assuming they enjoy checking out the new girl."

He continued to stare at her in silent expectation. Something intense flared through his dark eyes.

"What?" Totally bewildered at his behavior, Kayla let out a long, audible breath.

"Are you?"

Exasperated now, she let it sound in her voice. "Am I what?"

"My new girl?"

Momentarily abashed with heat stealing into her face, she rubbed the grout between the table tiles. He caught her hand between his, forcing her to look at him. "I'm so embarrassed," she began to explain. "I opened my mouth and inserted my foot. I didn't mean to imply…"

"Would you be?" He leaned forward and brushed a quick kiss against her lips.

She stared at him a moment, the idea so enticing and the kiss causing such a heady sensation she almost blurted out an instant "yes!" Her lips were still warm and moist from his and the connection filled a void that had been inside her for far too long. But a warning voice whispered in her head. She'd known him such a short time and she had her business to get off the ground. She couldn't afford to get sidetracked right now. But oh, how his interest cheered her on.

She saw her refusal reflected in his eyes before she ever spoke the words. "There is no one I'm more interested in furthering a relationship with than you. I love seeing you at the end of the day and I even manufacture ways to see you, like taking over your kitchen and cooking a meal without an invitation. In fact, that night I just wanted to hear your voice, experience your sense of humor." She reached for words that would explain how she felt yet at the same time not offend her companion. "But any relationship will need to be a gradual step by step, because right now I can't commit to anything more serious. Does that make sense?"

He took her other hand and rubbed the tops with his thumbs. "Perfect sense and I'm sorry for embarrassing you. I knew it was too soon to talk about a relationship, but the opportunity seemed right and I acted." His tone was apologetic but held a quiet emphasis.

She turned her palms and held his hands more securely. "I'm just starting Confetti. It requires so much of my time and you would become upset with me and I would not blame you." She thought for a moment as they sat in silence then added, "But I don't want to lose your friendship. Can we keep this on that level for the time being? You're very important to me, but right now that's all I have to give."

Marcelo slid out from under the cattle trailer, a satisfied feeling at his purchase. He'd never owned a gooseneck hauler before, always using his grandpa's tagalong. This was a huge thing and attached to a contraption inside his truck bed. He would be able to haul double the cattle. He needed to deliver a couple hundred to different auction houses in just a few weeks, so the timing was also perfect.

He couldn't always say that about his timing. He almost groaned aloud at the mess he'd made last Sunday. Things had been moving along smoothly and he'd gone and spoiled it. He knew the moment she rejected the idea. Her eyelids had closed over those beautiful, honey-brown eyes, closing her thoughts to him completely. He'd hastened to assure her that their circumstances were the same. That he didn't really have time for a serious relationship, either. He'd just moved into his new home a little over nine months ago, and even though he'd owned the ranch since his teens, he'd only taken possession of the place five years ago when his mother had divided the property among the three boys. He'd worked and saved and paid to get the house under roof. He'd then gotten a loan to finish and decorate the house as well as construct new barns and silos. His mortgage was huge but the sale of this year's cattle would cut it in half. Before the five years were up for the balloon payment he would be debt free, barring any complications and if the Lord so willed.

She had listened carefully to his explanation, then asked questions about his approach to modern-day ranching and grass-fed beef. He even saw excitement when she compared their goals and plans. As if she connected some common bond between them. They'd parted as friends; why he felt so dissatisfied and had so many misgivings, he didn't know. But he'd lain awake long into the night with a nagging in the back of his mind that would not be stilled.

Flipper joined him beside the trailer. "Want me to paint it for you, boss?"

Marcelo considered it for a moment. Black and shiny would look great on the metal. "No, not till after we deliver the cattle at the end of the month. Maybe then."

"The man delivered the bulldozer today."

Marcelo lifted his head, his serious mood suddenly

lightened. "Good. I think I'll get started on the road from here to the line shack."

"Sure thing, boss." Flipper turned to answer one of the men who had just parked the hay bailer. Marcelo used the opportunity to walk away and around the back of the barn. He'd wanted to clear Kayla's road since the day he'd put the lock on her door and she'd given him a hug. He climbed on the dozer, his mind full of possibilities for earning her gratitude once more.

Kayla turned onto the long drive to her house and immediately noticed the improvements to the road. No longer were there bumps and clumps of grass impeding her progress; just a smoother, wider road with a ditch on each side. She knew without asking that this was the work of one handsome Marcelo Fuentes. How she longed to drive on over to the ranch and thank him warmly, but she'd become uncomfortable thinking she'd been forward. She would, however, send him a note.

She carried clean laundry from the car to the house. She'd found a laundromat not far from Confetti and had become good friends with the owner. They did her clothes each week and until she could have her own washer and dryer installed, would continue to do so. The cost had not figured in her budget but for now she had to, as her mother used to say, "pay the piper."

She cleaned her house fervently, scrubbing the floors with detergent, cleaning the bath and lone window. Then she put the freshly washed sheets and bedspread on the bed. It took her all of an hour. She went outside, swept and sprayed off the porch with the water hose, and then washed the swing and chair. That took up a mere thirty minutes. The evening sun hadn't even cooled its rays. She looked toward the hacienda and wondered what Marcelo was doing. Was he having as hard a time staying away as she? He must have been thinking of her today at some point at least, because he had graded her road, making it pleasingly accessible and much easier on her car.

She walked around the back of the house and saw that the road from her house to his had been widened and the ruts completely removed. Her smile broadened in approval. It was like a sign. He had made it easier for her to come to him. That meant something, surely.

She went back in the house, indecision eating at her insides. Should she go over there and thank him? This was a huge favor he had done for her. She busied herself, trying to stifle the urge to go to him. She put her clean clothes into the plastic drawers she'd bought several weeks ago. Then she prepared her clothes for tomorrow. She was going to The Christmas House in Falfurrias with Alma and several of her friends in the church van. After much consideration, they had opened Confetti to the local businesses, churches and schools, but not to the public. This gave them a couple of month's trial and error as well as time to prepare for a spectacular grand opening day. Also, during this time of adjustment, Confetti was closed on Tuesdays and open from three to six in the afternoons on Wednesdays. The schedule was proving to be a "God-thing" as Alma called it because it gave them time to work on personal things, like a life.

She walked out onto the porch again, bored and frustrated. She sank onto the swing and wished that she liked to read, for at times like this it surely would come in handy. She relived Marcelo's kiss from last Sunday. She'd been surprised but her stomach did a flip-flop as she watched Marcelo's eyes close and felt the light brush of his lips. Her first kiss and he didn't even know.

She'd almost dozed off in the swing when she heard the sound of his diesel truck approaching from the back road. A cry of relief broke from her lips. She was so tired of the battle to keep her distance from him and was overjoyed to have the decision taken from her. She ran down the steps and met him as he climbed from the truck.

She said the first thing that came to mind. "I'm glad you're here." She could feel the same eager affection coming back from him.

"Do you like the road?" His gaze traveled over her face and searched her eyes. She saw the silent expectation and could no more refuse than she could deny herself breath.

"I absolutely love it," she enthused.

Teasing laughter filled his eyes. "What? No hug? I get hugged for a simple little lock on a door but just a few words for a hot day's work on a dozer?"

She almost danced into his arms and he lifted her and swung her around. He set her on her feet but kept his arms locked around her. "Now that's what I'm talking about." His gaze dropped from her eyes to her lips and she knew instinctively she wanted a kiss as much as he did. She lifted her mouth in mute appeal. He lowered his head, his kiss slow, thoughtful. He rested his brow against hers. "I've dreamed about that all day."

In that very moment her feelings for him intensified. She didn't know what was happening; it just simply felt right. He turned and guided her to the porch, but once there, he touched a finger to her cheek.

"Gotta go." Huskiness lingered in his voice.

"I know." Instead of disappointment, her nerves jangled with excitement. She'd gotten to see him and for some reason the restlessness in her soul had quieted.

"See you tomorrow?"

Amazed at the thrill his question gave her, she nodded. He turned and walked to the truck looking back over his shoulder.

She walked to the back of the house and watched till his taillights disappeared from view. She could rest now and plan her day for tomorrow.

The next morning Alma introduced Kayla to the occupants of the van, explaining briefly who they were. The girls her age were Carina Garza who had just gotten engaged and Adele Rivas who worked for Carina's fiancé's brother. There was the pastor's wife, Kim, and her friend DeAnn and several winter Texans. She'd never remember all the names right off the bat but hopefully by tomorrow she'd have them memorized.

They laughed and chatted on the hour-long drive north of the Rio Grande Valley. When they arrived they waited in the van, per instructions on the entrance gate, till one of the three owners came to admit them. Three senior-citizen sisters—never married retired schoolteachers—had turned their home into a showcase of decorated Christmas themes. They began on the carport and explained the decor and why it was chosen. Those who had chewing gum were asked to remove it before entering. Kayla chuckled aloud. This should be good.

The tour from room to room took about an hour and upon their return to the kitchen they were served a healthy snack. The tour then ended in the formal living room where the real reason for Christmas was displayed and explained. Christ was evident in the lives of the three Minten sisters. Kayla thoroughly enjoyed the storytelling, the songs and the camaraderie among the ladies. Then when they went to the old homeplace store that sold all the items showcased in the house, she really came alive. Alma had encouraged her to bring her checkbook and with good reason. Kayla quickly filled up a basket and took it to the counter and began on her second. Alma also added her choices with permission from Kayla, and together they purchased several items to make centerpieces for Christmas weddings and parties. The back of the van was piled high with their purchases, and the rest of the ladies teased them about hogging all the room.

On their way back to the valley the ladies began to question Carina about her fiancé and wedding. For a while Kayla listened intently to the plans and designs then her mind wandered to her own sweet Marcelo. How wonderful it had been to see him yesterday when with all her heart she longed to. And today was no different. But it didn't look like she would arrive home till late. The ladies were discussing the evening meal at a local restaurant and since Kayla's car was parked at the church she had no option but to go with them.

Her mind sprang back to the present. "What do you think, Kayla?" Alma's question threw her because she had no idea what they had talked about.

"I'm sorry? What did you say?"

Alma looked at her oddly and said under her breath, "Are you okay?"

She shook her head and asked again. "Carina wants to know what you think of purple and lime-green for wedding decor."

"Sounds lovely but the pictures will not be as vibrant."

"Oh, I hadn't thought of that. I remember a bridal shower I went to that had those colors and when the photos were returned, the purple was so light the lime green overpowered everything." Carina's voice sounded tired, broken with huskiness. Kayla suspected she was tired of all the hoopla that went into planning a wedding. She instinctively liked the young woman who was just one year older than she.

"What other colors have you considered?" Kayla decided to enter the conversation since Alma seemed to have tired of trying to sell Carina on the idea of allowing Confetti to cater the event.

Carina launched into the subject of colors, flowers, bridesmaids' dresses and wedding gowns. Kayla focused on her words, aware that at any moment she could start daydreaming about her own wedding. The nonexistent one, she reminded herself. Then suddenly the conversation took a different turn and she clued back in. "They're all three tall, dark and handsome. But mine is the best of the three." Carina broke into giggles and sounded like a little girl.

"Well, Marc is the funny one and that's a trait I like in a man." Adele added her two cents to the laughing group.

"But everyone knows, Adele, that you love Raoul. You can't hide it from us." Alma's voice held a curious teasing but sounded almost envious.

The pastor's wife, Kim, spoke next. "One good thing about those three brothers is they've all been faithful to the church. That's a good recommendation for husband material. Many young men their age are out sowing wild oats, but not them. So you single girls should reel them in while you can."

"Too true. Not many good guys left to choose from." Zelda, one of the winter Texans made a valid point. "Adele, what is the hold up with you and Raoul?"

"He needs to grow up and become a man before he's eligible for marriage." Adele's matter-of-fact tone let everyone know she knew what she was talking about. Kayla wondered briefly what this Raoul guy looked like and how Adele could be so in love with someone she hardly respected.

"What about you, Kayla?" Of all the ladies present, DeAnn had been the nicest to her, always trying to include her in their conversation. "Is there a tall, dark and handsome in your life?"

Kayla thought of Marcelo and wished she had someone special to talk to about him, but airing her concerns, desires and mostly wishful thinking with a group of ladies she'd just met was not something she felt comfortable with. "Not yet. My heart belongs to Confetti right now. Once my store is a success, I'll find my own tall, dark and handsome."

"Well, don't wait too long. Some lucky girl's going to come along and snatch the Fuentes brothers up." Kayla became instantly wide-awake at Kim's words. Fuentes brothers? And hadn't she heard the name Marc? Could they be talking about her Marcelo?

"Who are the Fuentes brothers?" She dug in her purse for the keys to the car, trying her best to appear nonchalant while she was anything but.

"They're local men who inherited citrus orchards near Padre Island. They each have other interests but the family business is citrus. Mainly grapefruit and oranges. And lemons but not so much those." Kim's explanation did nothing to relieve her curiosity. Marcelo raised cattle, not citrus, so maybe they were talking about another family. For all she knew Fuentes could be a common name in the valley. She turned to the seat behind her to further question Alma, but found her asleep with her face against the window. Oh, well, so much for that. She'd ask tomorrow evening.

But the next evening, thanks to word of mouth by Alma, they received two catering orders for private parties; one for a *Quinceañera* and the other for a sports group. Kayla helped one customer choose the menu and Alma finalized details with the other. The events were only two days apart so they spent the rest of the evening making a food list and pulling together decorations. They so needed a van but Kayla wanted to see a return before she invested that kind of money. This would definitely be a trial run but it would help to have this under their belt when they had the grand opening in two weeks.

A vague sense of unease had troubled her for the past several days. She couldn't quite put her finger on the cause and had little or no time to meditate and figure it out. But more and more it seemed Confetti didn't fill the little void in her heart where a loved one should be. Maybe she still grieved the loss of her parents, and thinking along those lines made her work harder. Surely it couldn't be that she longed for a relationship with Marcelo. She'd pretty much shot that down with her refusal to be his girl. But oh, how she wanted to be.

Chapter 5

Marcelo climbed astride his horse and took the reins for Kayla's horse from Flipper. He had plans. That he'd just invented another way to see her did not escape his notice, but he excused it as needing to show her what she owned. That was a necessity in his eyes. She stepped out on the porch as he rode up, and his heart did an oddly primitive dance.

"What's up, neighbor?" Even her voice filled him with tenderness.

"I thought it was time you saw your inheritance and there's no better way to cover the acreage than on a horse." He held the reins out to her. "Ever been on one of these?"

"Once when I was a child. But it was a pony, not a huge horse that looks like it might run away with me."

She remained on the porch, not even attempting to take the reins. He felt his smile widen.

"You're not afraid, are you?"

"Well of course I am."

"Really?" he teased. "Bessie is the calmest, coolest mare I have and she would never run away with you."

"Bessie? Isn't that a name for a cow?" She came down the first step. Her voice was full of derision but he saw the struggle in her face. She didn't back down from a challenge and he guessed she really wanted to see her land. He should have brought the four-wheeler. That way she could have ridden with him and her arms would have gone around his waist. He almost groaned aloud at the missed opportunity to have her close.

He dismounted and held out his hand. She put her foot in the stirrup and sat the horse like a professional. Then she messed it all up by grabbing his arm.

"Don't go fast, okay?"

He squeezed her hand encouragingly. "I promise we'll take it slow." His mouth said one thing; he hoped his eyes reminded her of their conversation the day he'd asked her if she'd be his girl. He'd told her then that they'd keep it slow. He wondered if she remembered.

They rode along the fence line till they came to a cattle crossing and then went down to her pond.

"Oh, law. This is horrible. How did it get so messed up?"

Water bottles and trash floated on green algae. Debris lined the land around the water and deep pock marks lined one side where the cattle went in to drink.

"Before we fenced in this section of your land, people could roam this area freely. Hunters, illegals passing through and many of your neighbors used this as a picnic area. Over time, it became a trash dump and has never been cleaned up."

"Can it even be cleaned up? This seems like a monumental task."

"Professionals will have to do it now with a backhoe or dozer. You'll need a dump truck to haul the trash off." Marcelo saw the look of utter defeat cross her face. "It's not impossible and even though it's a major job, it can be completed in a day's time."

"And the cost will be phenomenal, right?"

"Depends on whether or not you're nice to your neighbor." He spaced the words evenly and wasn't disappointed at the look of surprise on her face.

"You can do this kind of work?"

"I can't haul it off, but I can remove the trash and shore up the sides of the pond so that the dirt doesn't keep washing into the water. It needs a new reservoir built to store the water so it doesn't evaporate during the hot summer days, but it's not such an impossible task as one might think."

"And what can I do to help?" She looked him straight in the eye and he liked that about her. She faced problems head-on and nothing seemed to shake her. His thoughts scampered vaguely around as he held her steady gaze. Did she ever have moments of doubt? Was she afraid of being a failure? It didn't seem to be part of her makeup and he looked forward to finding these things out about her. He sensed she would not appreciate a flippant answer to her question about helping.

It was her property and she wanted to be in control of what happened. He understood that more than perhaps even she. He liked it.

"Well, you can supervise."

"Job title without actual work, huh? Not interested."

"Good girl." He turned to look at the pond. "We need to find where the actual water feed is and start there so that we don't mess up the natural spring feeding the pond, but I think if you had a crew of volunteers collecting trash on the banks and someone strong clearing the brush and tumbleweed it would speed things up and be a big help."

Without hesitation, she responded positively. "I can do that. But I'll be happy to pay anyone who helps. As long as it doesn't bankrupt me."

They rode to the property line and he helped her dismount.

"So this is my land?"

"Such as it is, yes."

She turned to look at him and he regretted his response when all the intensity of her gaze was switched to him. "What does that mean?"

"Well, for one, your land is surrounded by mine. You have no access unless I grant you right-of-way." He deliberately baited her and for reasons he didn't fully understand.

He watched a gamut of perplexing emotions cross her face, and he felt like a heel. Still, he excitedly waited for her response. Even if she were angry at him, he loved experiencing the feelings running riot inside him.

"I don't already have a right-of-way access to my land?"

"Not on paper. My granddad shook hands with your grandpa years ago. That was all the legalities needed back then."

"Our grandparents were friends?"

They strolled along the fence line, holding to the reins of the horses. They could see her property for miles around but Marcelo noticed neither of them even glanced at it.

"Very good friends from the stories I've been told."

"Did you know my mother?"

"No, I never met her, but there are photos of her and my mother playing together when they were smaller. Would you like to see them sometime?"

"I would love to."

"Then I'll fix dinner one evening and you can look through the family photo albums to your heart's content." He said the words tentatively as if testing the idea.

"I'd love that."

He took her hand. She didn't resist and that made his heart soar.

"Are you very close to your family, Marcelo?"

"We're a close-knit clan. My brothers and I fought off and on growing up but that's pretty normal, I'm told. We spent a lot of time away from our dad because he had to keep the family plantation in Mexico running, but he came to see us and we went there as often as we could. That was difficult, especially for Juan Antonio. Lack of communication seems to be a problem in our family, and in fact, it almost cost him his fiancée."

Surprised again, Kayla felt a soft gasp escape her. "Juan Antonio Fuentes is your brother?" Without waiting for a response she plowed on. "And I bet you have a brother named Raoul, and he's in love with Adele Rivas, right?"

"Well, I wouldn't go that far. I think Raoul is in love with himself more than Adele, but yes, they're my brothers. How did you know?" She could have laughed out loud at the look on his face.

"When we went to Falfurrias the other week, the girls were talking about the famous Fuentes men and their flaws or lack thereof. I wondered if they were any relation to you. Someone even mentioned Marc, but I didn't realize it was you." She touched the front of his shirt close to his heart. "Now I wish I'd paid more attention. I might have found out something about you."

"You know all the important stuff already." He caught her hand and kept it pressed to his chest.

"Like what? I don't really know anything at all." He gave her a look of utter disbelief.

"How can you say that, Kayla? I'm wounded."

She rolled her eyes at his exaggeration. "I know you're my neighbor, that you feed my cattle, that you know more about my family than I do and that you drive a honking big diesel truck." She pulled her hands free and placed them on her hips. "For all I know you could be an ax murderer."

"Ah, Kayla." He placed an arm across her shoulders and started them walking again. "If you're my neighbor and I feed your cattle what does that say about me?" When she just looked at him and refused to answer, he continued in a voice meant to convince. "It says I'm a nice, kind neighbor. If I know your family and they've never once mentioned a crazy ax murderer neighbor then quite possibly I'm not one. And my diesel only says I have good taste." He pulled her into a tight arm hold and spoke into her ear. "And the fact that your eyes light up when you see me says your heart likes me whether your mind does or not, right?"

Kayla was impressed with the confidence he inspired in her to open up to him. Even with her parents, she'd never felt such freedom to speak her mind. Searching for a plausible answer to his last question, she decided to take a chance and be honest with him. "I do feel extreme happiness when I see you, and I miss you when I don't. I'm very happy we're friends, but I would love to know more about you. For instance, your parents. Where do they live? Do you have sisters? Been married before? There are just a few areas of information missing." She grinned at him and raised her eyebrows in question. His arm around her shoulders made it impossible to walk comfortably so she placed an arm about his waist and immediately doubted her actions.

"No sisters. Daddy passed away almost two years ago and Mother lives here in the winter and spends the summer months in the cooler mountains. Never been married. No illegitimate children. And I'd like to explore this extreme happiness you mentioned."

"And I'm just getting started. I want to know your favorite color, favorite foods, restaurants, your political views and if you're a player."

"What's a player?"

"A man who loves women and tries to have more than one interested in him at one time. He talks to all of them as if they're his gal and doesn't really settle on a certain one."

"Would you be jealous if I were like that?"

"No. I wouldn't see you at all if you were like that. Do you think bad of me because I asked you that?"

"No, not really. I hope I've not given you reason to think that of me, and I hope this is not coming from a past experience you've had with a man."

"Actually it comes from the messages from Song of Solomon that Pastor preached the past few Sundays. Remember he said the Shulamite, when she first started a relationship with Solomon, was very insecure and needed constant reassuring? I guess I feel a little like that when I'm with you."

"What do you mean?"

"Well, just that I'm happy, happy one minute with you, and the next I'm feeling uncertain if you feel the same way, or if I'm reading the signals all wrong. I know we agreed to just be friends, but sometimes it feels like we're more. At least to me it does."

"Okay, let me answer your question. I am not a player. There are no other women in my life other than my mother, Carina, Juan Antonio's fiancée and Adele, who serves as my housekeeper as well as Raoul's. You—" he tilted her chin up to look directly into her eyes "—invade my thoughts constantly and I have all the symptoms you just mentioned. So I guess we could safely say the feelings are mutual. Now what if we see where these feelings take us?" He brushed a wayward strand of hair behind her ear.

The idea appealed tremendously to Kayla and she couldn't deny the spark of excitement at the prospect. But they'd known each other for such a short time and she felt a small voice saying "wait." Her sensible side replied, "There's a temptation to move too fast, Marc. Let's just take it easy and see how things go." She wondered if all the Fuentes men were so impulsive when it came to relationships.

Chapter 6

"Mom, where are you jetting off to so soon?" Marcelo could hear the exasperation in his voice and he fought to remain calm. As the oldest of the brothers, he felt it his duty to keep track of his mom and her many adventures. His mother was fifty-three, for goodness' sake. Wasn't it time she settled down and quit running around so much? "You just got here yesterday and you're leaving already? Shouldn't you rest up a day or two at least?"

Marta Fuentes strolled into the bedroom from her private bathroom carrying toiletries she placed in the suitcase she'd unpacked only yesterday. She clicked the latches shut then lifted it, testing its weight. She set it on the floor apparently satisfied it wasn't too heavy to pull through the airport terminal.

"Would you hand me that Caboodle, dear, and I'll pack my cosmetics." Marta placed the few items that lay on the bed into the lime-green carrier. "Oh, where is my eyebrow pencil? Lord knows I'll need that." She located the item and then looked up into his eyes. She was such a petite little person; she always made him feel like a giant. She barely stood four foot nine inches, had perfect, shoulder-length, curly, salt-and-pepper hair. "I've been invited to go on a trip with your Tia Yvette and I'm going. We'll only be gone a week and it's perfectly safe. We won't be going out in the pueblos of Cancun, but will stay in the tourist areas. You don't need me here, son, so what's your concern?"

"I thought you came to spend time with us. Your sons. Remember us?" Marcelo's statement seemed to irritate her to no end. And he knew she would accuse him of trying to make her feel guilty. But if there was one thing he knew about his mother, it was that she answered to no man. She'd had enough of that to last her a lifetime and her sons sure weren't going to boss her around. After all, as she'd said many times, *"I gave you life, and I can take it from you."*

"It's just for a week, Marcelo, and I will be here for six months."

"That's another thing you haven't told me yet. Why are you here in July? You usually don't arrive till September." His mother had shown up unexpectedly, and though she was welcome anytime, this was odd. That she had come to the hacienda first instead of to the Citrus Queen sure seemed suspicious, as well. Something was up but he doubted she'd clue him in until she was good and ready.

"Okay, I guess I do owe you an explanation." She sat

down in a chair and patted the side of the bed. "Sit here and I'll tell you a story. Remember when I used to tell you boys stories at night?" Her voice was soothing as it had been the many times in their tumultuous good-byes to their father, who refused to leave his precious mango plantation in Mexico.

"That was twentysome-odd years ago, Mom." He sat down and looked expectantly at the one constant thing in his life. She was the most precious woman he knew. He would not know what to do without her and suspected she lived up north during the summer months just so her sons wouldn't hover around her, treating her like china.

"I know, but those were good memories." She looked away as if remembering a different lifetime.

"And the reason you're here early…" he prompted.

"Remember that I was late leaving for the summer this year and didn't get out of here till the end of April? Well, that was God's timing because Juan Antonio needed help straightening some things out. He wanted to marry sweet Carina without carrying so much baggage from the past into his new life with her. Well, I felt I was needed here again, and though I'm not sure why, God in his infinite wisdom does. So I followed his prompting and here I am."

"Now, why do I feel you're not telling the whole truth, *Mamacita?*" Marcelo knew a con when he saw one, and though what she said had a ring of truth to it, something clearly wasn't right.

"I never could pull the wool over your eyes, could I, Markie?" She knew he hated that nickname and used it just so he would get upset and leave her alone. Oh, yes, he knew all her little ploys and wasn't falling for any of them.

"No, you couldn't, and I wish you'd stop trying to now. So, out with it." He allowed a warning cloud to settle on his features. She wasn't the only one who knew how to manipulate. "Should I call J.T. and Raoul?" He used the shortened version of Juan Antonio's name.

"Oh, all right. I guess I can tell you—but only if you keep my confidence." At his nod she continued. "I met a man and I know he loves me, but I'm not sure I want a relationship with him."

"Why not?" Marcelo felt like he'd been sucker punched but allowed no expression to cross his features. He could not imagine his mother with anyone other than his dad.

"Well…" She wrung her hands. "Charlie doesn't want to travel. His heart's desire is to marry me, become a winter Texan and retire on South Padre Island. Truth be told, I'd be happy as a pea in a pod to settle down again because traveling and eating in different restaurants keeps me from getting the fiber in my diet that I need for proper gut maintenance. And you know that intestinal problems cause a person my age to become quite cranky."

Seeing the amusement in her eyes, he laughed. "Way too much information, Mother. Now cut to the chase."

Her humorous words accomplished the desired effect on Marcelo. He relaxed his rigid posture and adapted a much nicer attitude. She had worked him like that since he was five years old and decided he was the man of the house and could boss her around. He loved her dearly but that didn't mean he wasn't wise to her ways.

"And he's such a good man. You're going to love him, Marcelo. He has so many cool stories and he takes such good care of me."

"So what's the problem?"

"It feels odd to think of someone else in my life other than your dad. Almost as if I were cheating on your father, you know?" She hugged her arms to her in a protective action.

"Seems to me if you loved this guy you wouldn't even be thinking of Dad. He's been gone how long now? Two years?"

"Only sixteen months, my dear, and I do love Charlie. I do."

"But Dad was bedridden for a couple of years after the stroke so it seems longer than sixteen months." He stretched his long legs in front of him, suddenly uncomfortable with the direction the conversation had taken. Finally it dawned on him that she was still beating around the bush. "So if you love him so much just what is the reason you're having doubts?"

She went back to wringing her hands, and refused to look him in the eyes, but at last she gave him an answer. "He's forty-seven."

Marcelo nearly fell off the bed. "Forty-seven? And you're fifty-three?" His voice had raised an octave. "That's six years' difference, Mom, and you're the older one."

"I know. Is that really so bad, though? Women so often outlive their husbands. I have friends who've been widows for years. So my being older can't be a bad thing, right? Besides, he loves me and knows nothing about my money. He wants to take care of me. He retired from the air force and then retired from the state as a teacher. He is financially independent and very smart. His wife passed away with cancer several years ago and like me, he hates being alone."

"Then put the man out of his misery and marry him."

She jumped up from her seat, happiness shining from her eyes. "Really, Marcelo? You won't hate me for replacing your dad?"

"Whoa." He held up both hands. "He will never take the place of Dad, so don't be thinking we're going to call him that."

"I didn't mean it like that. I just meant he would be the man in my life, not your dad."

"Then you have my blessing, Mom, if that's what you're looking for."

She stretched on tiptoes to give him a hug and he gathered her close. He would hate sharing her but knew she was still young enough to enjoy being married again. As he turned her loose she sighed heavily.

"Now what's wrong?"

"I hate sharing all my gut maintenance problems with a new guy. How embarrassing. Why, just the other day after eating at a certain Italian restaurant, I had to stop at McDonalds and use the bathroom. I couldn't even make it home."

"Mom, I don't want to hear it, either."

"Well you should, Markie. It may be inherited. Do you go potty every day?"

"Mooooom," he warned.

"Well, it's important. You feel so much better if you do and who else can you talk about these kinds of problems with if not your mother?"

He grabbed the handle of her luggage and called over his shoulder. "I'll be in the car whenever you're ready."

"Now, there's a good boy." He was so gullible. Kids these days thought older people lacked intelligence, but his mom still knew how to clear a room.

Marta left the bedroom, a light coat slung over her shoulder, a little dance in her step. Marcelo knew she loved the institution of marriage. As she'd explained to them many times, to her way of thinking, two heads were better than one. Caring for and loving a husband was an honor and one she'd carried out with unswerving devotion. She'd said at the graveside that she regretted a lot of things as she said goodbye to her first love, but repeated that she'd do it all again without any doubt if she could have him back.

Marcelo opened her door as she approached and the thought crossed his mind that he needed to spend some quality time with her when she returned from Cancun.

"Let's go, child. The sooner I get this over with, the sooner I can spoil my man to pieces." Little did she know that those were Marcelo's thoughts also. Soon he would be back and he'd get to see the beautiful Kayla. Life was good.

The month of July came and went. The grand opening was a huge success. The only sad part was Marcelo couldn't attend. He'd traveled to an auction in New

Mexico with two trailers of cattle. But Kayla had gone to church with him every Sunday since the first time he invited her, and had gotten to know quite a few of the people. Alma regularly invited her to church but Kayla told her she was happy where she was at.

She'd told Alma about Mr. Fuentes repairing her road and how he brought her food on the nights she worked late. They had so little time together but it was enough to give her hope that things might eventually work out between them. There'd been no more kisses and she longed for that closeness with him that she'd barely been given a taste of.

But Confetti bypassed her wildest dreams and she was making a substantial profit. She drew up plans for an addition to her house, nothing extravagant but something that would make her little home more livable. The same man who often helped with construction work at Confetti had agreed to do the addition at minimal cost, and the materials would be delivered in the next couple of days. Even with all this excitement, something was still missing from her life.

Regularly she poured her heart out to God, receiving comfort for the moment, but the emptiness remained. Only when she was in the presence of Marcelo did she feel completely happy. Was this love?

Marcelo stared at Kayla sleeping soundly on his porch. She lay in the swing, her arms crisscrossed over her stomach. One leg hung over the side as if to prevent a sudden spill, should she turn in her sleep. He grinned and gently pushed the metal chain that attached the swing to the roof, unintentionally setting in motion an avalanche of disaster.

A horrific shriek rent the air, arms flailed, legs kicked, then she landed with a thump on the plank floor. Surprise then anger twisted her features as she scrambled to her feet.

"You big baboon. What did you do that for?" She clenched her fists by her side and jutted her chin forward. It reminded him of the day she'd threatened him with mace.

Marcelo's shoulders shook, though he tried hard to conceal his mirth. He bent and grabbed his knees, uncontainable laughter causing tears to form in his eyes. He fought for control.

"You looked so funny," he admitted.

"I'm happy to have provided your evening entertainment, Mr. Fuentes. Now, if you'll excuse me."

Marcelo halted her escape with a hand on her arm.

"Wait, Kayla." He backtracked quickly. "I didn't mean for you to fall. You seemed pretty well entrenched in that thing. I only wanted to wake you."

"Well, you succeeded." She turned to enter the line shack.

"What's with the building supplies out back?"

She paused at his question then looked over her shoulder. "Mr. Fuentes, I realize that you're the one who feeds and waters my livestock and I appreciate it. But that doesn't give you license to invade my privacy. The building supplies are none of your business."

"Kayla, listen, I'm sorry for dumping you from the swing." Marcelo allowed humility to enter his voice.

"Don't hold a grudge. It's a beautiful Sunday afternoon, and one of us even got a nap." He watched her shoulders relax, and he smiled.

"Come on," he encouraged. "Show me what's out back."

Marcelo knew the moment she relented; excitement shone in her honey-flecked eyes. His heartbeat tripled at her soft laugh. The color of her hair reminded him of the wheat fields on his ranch, ready for harvest. He hurried down the steps after her and stopped about nine feet from the corner of the building.

"See this flat rock?" Barely waiting for his nod, she continued. "Stand on it."

She pulled his arm until he stood where she wanted him. She counted aloud as she stepped off twenty-four paces then turned to face him.

"This is the width of the new addition. The back wall will be flush with the house. I'm adding a living room and a bedroom to the existing bath and kitchen. One room gets a little crowded after a while. Oh, and look." She paced another twelve steps, arms extended. "Right here will be a floor-to-ceiling window." She pointed opposite where she stood. "Here also. I wanted a fireplace in between, but the expense—oh, well, the builders say they'll add one later if I want."

"Kayla…"

"The man said he could have the roof on by next Saturday if the cement people finish on time. They're pouring the footers and floor tomorrow after lunch. Do you think it will be dry by Tuesday morning?" Without waiting for an answer she hurried on excitedly. "I'm going to have hardwood floors so I can use rugs. And I've ordered a central air unit. The company that installed the one at Confetti says they'll outfit the kitchen and bath as well as the new addition. No more roaring from that little window unit."

Her words hit him like a shower of pebbles, robbing him of speech. He realized his mistake. He should have told her sooner. His silence was going to cost him dearly. Searching for a plausible explanation, he ran a hand over the back of his neck.

"Oh, Marc. I'm so happy. For the first time in my life I'm putting down permanent roots. I'm finally going to have a home." She swung around and smiled up at him, happiness radiating from every pore, unaware she'd shortened his name for the first time.

For the space of a couple of heartbeats he forgot to breathe. He stared, enchanted by the woman in front of him. Joy bubbled in her laughter. Even her walk had a sunny cheerfulness. He never wasted a second thought about his response to her, or the protective feelings rising within him. They came naturally. A sudden uncomfortable twist of his conscience brought him up short.

"Well?" she asked impatiently. "What do you think?"

Static, a series of clicks, then Flipper's voice interrupted them. "Boss? You there?"

Marcelo pushed the button on the walkie-talkie clipped on his belt. "Go ahead, Flip." He released the button, waiting for the other man's response.

"Boss, you're not going to like this, but that crazy woman living in your line shack had David West draw up a floor plan. The materials have already been delivered. She's going to add on to the line shack. Can you believe that?"

Marcelo watched a riot of expressions cross Kayla's face. Her smile that just moments before had equaled the sun, faded. A momentary look of confusion, then pain, filled her eyes. A second more and comprehension dawned.

"Boss? Are you there?"

Marcelo clicked the two-way radio's off button, his black eyes never leaving the stricken ones staring back at him. He lifted a hand toward her as a hoarse cry escaped her lips.

"What did he mean *your* line shack?" Then her eyes widened. "Line shack?"

"Kayla." He touched her arm, but she yanked away from him.

"This is my land." Her brows drew together in an agonized expression. "Isn't it?" Her voice was full of entreaty. "And the lawyers—" she swallowed "—they said there was a small structure. Surely they didn't mean that shack that's falling down...." Her voice faded at his nod. "But the roof is missing, so I thought..."

Marcelo's stomach churned and a sense of inadequacy swept over him. In his gut, he knew this woman was important to his happiness.

"Our boundary lines join at that clump of mesquite trees." Marcelo pointed. "We built the line shack about four years ago, after Hurricane Alfred swept through and flooded the area."

"And you let me move in, live here all this time and didn't say a word. How you guys must have laughed.

Well, this 'crazy woman,' won't be a problem for you anymore." She turned away, not waiting for an answer.

"Where are you going, Kayla?" When she didn't slow her headlong flight toward the house, he ran after her.

He entered the shack on her heels and stared helplessly as she filled two suitcases with her belongings.

"What are you doing?" He stepped between her and the clothes she reached for next. "You don't have to leave. Why can't you stay here? You've made it your home."

She moved away from him; her arms hugged her body in a protective gesture. "Why did you let me live here? Why did you make a fool out of me? All this time.... Why?"

"You latched on to the place like a drowning person to a life raft. I knew you'd just lost your parents and might not have a place to go. I offered to buy your land. I thought if you needed money for a place to live you'd jump at my offer. But you ran me off the property. Threatened me with mace and the police. I didn't have the heart to take this away from you. I still don't. Please stay, Kayla."

"No. I have to go." She stepped around him and grabbed the last of her clothes from the dresser.

Marcelo followed her to the car but nothing he said persuaded her to stay. He watched the red convertible disappear down the track, misery weighing heavily in his soul.

Chapter 7

Homeless again!

Kayla turned slowly, her gaze roaming the multifarious party supplies hanging in neat rows from ceiling to floor. She waited for the familiar sense of tranquility the store usually generated to settle over her. Confetti belonged to her. No one could take it away. Marcelo's remark from yesterday had swirled round and round in her mind. *You latched on to the place like a drowning person to a life raft.* Those words struck so close to home she could almost feel the panic. That sinking, grasping feeling of hanging on by the fingernails was the story of her life.

"Are you okay?"

Kayla whirled to face the current source of her distress. Preoccupied with jumbled thoughts, she hadn't heard Marcelo enter the store.

She said the first thing that came into her mind. "We're not open yet."

"I've been sick with worry. Where were you?" Marcelo touched her shoulder then his hand slid down her arm and clutched her wrist. "I circled by here twice last night then searched all over town for you."

Kayla studied him carefully. His face, bronzed by the wind and sun, revealed an inherent strength. The shadow of his beard gave him a manly aura. His mouth, usually parted in a dazzling display of straight white teeth, was pulled tight by the muscle clenched along his jaw. Worry lined his brow. Something inside her cheered up for a moment. It felt good to have someone care about her. But he still had a few things to answer for. Her self-made safety mechanism for *you're not allowed to hurt me,* perfected down through the years, must be faulty. Without the least bit of warning, he'd slipped through. And he'd hurt her.

"You know, Mr. Fuentes, you're an imposter. You present yourself as an honest, decent, caring man. But in reality you lied to me, laughed at me and made a fool of me. So pardon me if I see you as a fraud."

"I've never lied to you."

"You don't call keeping the truth from someone a lie?" Kayla lowered her voice an octave. "It's the same thing. And each time we met, you invited me to church. What for? So I could be like you? Thanks, but no thanks." Kayla knew she hit below the belt but the hurt in her wanted to lash out at someone, to make him suffer the same losses as she.

"That's not fair and you know it. I…"

He paused as the bell over the door jingled and Alma entered, calling out happily as she approached. "Kayla, you left your cell phone at the apartment this morning. Oh, hi, Marc. Missed you at church last night. Have you started working on Sunday nights or something? You've missed a lot lately."

"You know him?"

"You work here?"

Marc and Kayla spoke simultaneously. Alma glanced from one to the other then piled her purse, car keys and Kayla's cell phone on the checkout counter before answering.

"Yes, I know him. I went to school with him. I go to church with him, and my Tio Felipe works for him." She turned to look at *him*. "And, yes, Marc, I work here."

"Then why haven't you mentioned that you knew each other?" Kayla fought to keep the accusation from her voice.

"Why would I? I mean, I wasn't aware the two of you were acquainted."

"Alma, what are you talking about? I have complained…." Kayla paused midsentence, unsure why she found it difficult to insult this man in front of someone else.

Alma frowned, then her eyes widened in surprise.

"So this is the Mr. Fuentes who tried to buy you out. I didn't make the connection. You never used his given name. Anyway, you made him sound so old. Mr. Fuentes indeed." Alma grinned as if that cleared everything up.

"But I've gone with him to church for weeks now and I've never seen you."

"I have nursery on Sunday mornings. You should come back on Sunday nights. I'm in the front row of the choir. You couldn't miss me."

Marcelo had wandered off during their exchange. As if to top the insanity, he spun around and exclaimed, "Wow! I didn't realize this place was so big and impressive!"

Kayla stared at him as if he'd grown two heads. His glance darted from one wall to the other. He walked between the aisles, disappearing from sight. His voice carried back to them. "There's enough junk in here to last forever. I thought you just planned parties and sold specialty foods. With all this stuff people can plan their own parties. What would they need you for?"

"Well, you see—" Alma trotted along behind him "—that's what's unique about Confetti. We offer it all. Customers may buy their own theme, and if they have questions or need help, we supply it. If the party's on a grander scale, then we plan the details and cater it. We do anniversary dinners, *Quinceañeras,* wedding rehearsals and just last month we planned the new Christian radio station's open house. It was so much fun."

"What a great marketing idea."

Until now, Kayla had been simmering over the *junk* remark, but the awed respect in Marcelo's voice revitalized her senses. He stopped in front of her and completely disarmed her with a slow smile. His dark eyes were as beautiful as black satin.

"You're onto something here, Kayla. This is great."

Kayla wanted to remain aloof, but the delayed gratification concerning Confetti gave her intense joy. Confetti was her baby, her pride. Conceived from a heart deprived of simple pleasures like birthday parties. Designed and created with the eagerness of a child on Christmas morning. Paid for by the only permanent thing her parents ever gave her: a life-insurance policy. Barring any unforeseen disaster, Confetti would be her children's heritage. She would never, ever, yearn for a party again.

"Thank you, Mr. Fuentes."

Avoiding his gaze, she glanced at Alma, who stared back, raised eyebrows and slightly open mouth a sure sign she'd just experienced an epiphany.

"I'll see you this afternoon?" Marcelo's voice soothed yet insisted.

Unwilling to commit, she murmured, "We'll see." She refused to admit how much his lowered voice affected her, the mellow baritone sweeping along her already sensitized nerves.

"Later, Alma," he called over his shoulder.

"See you, Marc."

Kayla watched until he drove away then faced Alma's knowing look. "What?"

Alma took on the dreaded defensive stance, crossing her arms across her chest and shifting her weight to one leg. "Oh, don't *what* me, Kayla Guerrero. You're attracted to that man, and he's in over his head with you."

"Oh, yeah, right. That's why I'm out of house and home. Because he loves me."

"No, Kayla. I watched the two of you. The room ricocheted with tension. Don't you see? That's why he repaired the driveway so your sports car wouldn't drag." Alma carried on excitedly, as if in dawning comprehension. "He feeds your animals every day, cuts the hay in your pasture. If he hasn't fallen for you already, then he's well on his way."

Kayla turned on the computer and placed Alma's things under the counter. "You're wrong, Alma. He just wants my land and my water rights. That's why he let me live in his line shack and conveniently forgot to tell me it wasn't my house. He probably wanted me close by to impress me with what a nice guy he is so I would want to sell. Who could refuse Mr. Wonderful? And all that time I thought he was being kind and helpful."

"Shows how little you know Marc Fuentes." Alma walked to the front and switched on the open sign.

"Then tell me what I don't know about him," Kayla invited.

"Well, I'm not sure I have all the facts, but Marcelo's mother is Hispanic-American and his dad was a Mexican national. He has two brothers, Juan Antonio, and Raoul—both younger than him. You met Carina when we went to The Christmas House and she's engaged to the middle brother, Juan Antonio. By the way, Carina finally signed a contract the other day and we're doing the decorations at the rehearsal dinner. I think I have her hooked. Just need to reel her in slowly." Satisfaction pursed her mouth at a job well done. "Anyway, about Marc…"

"I know all that about his brothers and Carina, but do you know his mother?"

"Yes. During our school years I saw her a lot, but I haven't seen her much in the past few years. She doesn't go to our church or anything. And she's only here during the winter anyway."

"Mr. Fuentes and I have a lot in common."

"You do?" Without waiting for an answer, Alma rushed on. "Why do you call him *Mister?* That's one reason I didn't make the connection. When you say *Mister* I think of someone much older. He's the same age as me, and you don't call me Miss Cantu."

"Mostly to aggravate him and keep him at arm's length."

"So you admit he gets to you."

"Will you quit matchmaking?"

"Okay, okay. Did you get all your phone calls made?"

"Yes. I canceled the cement. Called the company to return the building supplies and informed the contractor." Kayla grimaced. "They weren't very happy with me."

"I'm sorry about your house, Kayla. I know how much the new addition meant to you."

"Thanks, Alma. I'll get over it. I always do."

For the first time in ten years, Marcelo longed to spin his tires, sling gravel and leave black marks a half mile long. Frustration had steadily built inside him since he heard Flipper's voice over the walkie-talkie yesterday. The situation had escalated out of his control in a matter of seconds. Hurt, Kayla had left his property, and he was to blame. When he'd found her at the store, he hid his annoyance over her disappearance. He'd worried all through the night, sleeping very little. Thoughts of danger crossed his mind. But the sight that caused his uncustomary need for antacids was Kayla's eyes rimmed in tears as she'd whispered goodbye.

He passed the Edinburg City Limit sign and pushed the cruise button on the steering wheel. It took twenty minutes' driving before he reached the turnoff to the ranch, then fifteen minutes more before he came to the line-shack road. He allowed his mind free rein as the fields rolled past his window.

Kayla had suppressed her anger the moment Alma appeared. He felt a smile crinkle the corners of his eyes. That could only mean she wanted to keep what passed between them private. He liked that. He'd had a girlfriend once who excelled at public arguments. She'd gotten her kicks from making him appear small in front of others. He'd thought he was in love. What he felt for Kayla seemed light-years away from the mere affection he'd held for his old girlfriend. However, thanks to the old flame, he knew he wasn't in love with Kayla, either. At least he'd figured that out last night. He didn't deny that he felt compassion and protectiveness, along with a strong attraction. What man wouldn't be attracted to a beautiful, warm and fun woman like Kayla? And they'd both said they wanted to get to know each other better, to explore where the relationship might go. But that wasn't love. No, what he felt couldn't be love.

Marcelo turned onto the line-shack road, crossed the cattle guard and continued past the ruins of the adobe house that was part of Kayla's inheritance. He parked his Ford F350 crew cab diesel pickup beside a Chevrolet Cheyenne half-ton truck and grinned at the sudden urge to execute a manly *argh, argh, argh,* because his truck was bigger, sturdier and more powerful.

"Marc." David West hurried toward him, his expression revealing his aggravation. "What's going on here? I get calls to proceed, then calls to stop. My orders are countermanded, and my men have no clear instructions. I thought this place belonged to a Miss Guerrero."

Marcelo shut the door of his truck and walked into the shade of the line shack, his hand on David's shoulder. "I'm sorry, ol' man, but let me straighten things out for you."

Thirty minutes later, Marcelo strolled into his house, the high ceilings, terra-cotta tiled floor and central air tempting him to lay his tired body on the huggable leather sofa and sleep until logic and reason returned. *You have no time,* a warning voice whispered in his head. *She'll go to lunch at twelve.* In the kitchen he removed a jug of tea from the refrigerator, tipped the rim to his mouth and drank, the cool liquid quenching his thirst. He glanced at the clock above the breakfast nook. Ten minutes past eleven. Just enough time to drive back to Confetti. He recapped the jug and shut the refrigerator door. He looked around the huge rooms, more certain than ever that he was on the right track. Now to set it all in motion.

Back in the truck, with the air conditioner set at full blast, he perfected the plan he had formulated just before dawn this morning. Kayla's ways, her smiles and her bubbly happiness intrigued him. For months now, he'd listened to her chatter on and on about Confetti, and watched her eyes light up when she spoke of putting down roots. She presented herself as a woman of the world, a businesswoman. She drove a Mercedes convertible and wore clothing he felt sure came right off the cover of those women's magazines. Yet she'd had no compunction about moving into a one-room line shack, with a bathroom that resembled an outhouse with electricity and running water. What had that been all about?

Marcelo knew he had a talent for problem solving. He always cared for the underdog and could spot someone in need a mile away. That's why Kayla seemed so important to him: she had broken dreams in her life. He had no idea the extent of them, but he sensed they were there. He could fix them. He'd arrived at this conclusion last night. He'd read his Bible, hoping for some relief. *And now abideth faith, hope, charity, these three; but the greatest of these is charity.*

He'd actually been excited at the thought that he might be in love with Kayla, but he'd felt fear, too. Love rendered a man powerless. Then it dawned on him that since they'd first met, she'd needed him for one thing or another. He felt God had spoken to him through that verse. He thought of the plaque Kayla tacked on the line-shack door the day she arrived. *As for me and my house, we will serve the Lord.* Marcelo would help strengthen her faith, create new hope and give his time and talent till Kayla no longer needed him. That it was hard to remain coherent when he was close to her didn't seem to register; at least if it did he brushed it aside.

He pulled into the lot at Confetti, confidence restored and plans coming together. He was a man on a mission.

* * *

Kayla and Alma worked quietly together, occasionally comparing notes about upcoming events and parties. Around eleven, both women opened boxes of inventory. While Kayla computed invoices, Alma hung latex balloons on the wall. Kayla worried silently over the situation she found herself in.

Like Marcelo's dad, Kayla's father also was a Mexican national. The difference was he lived illegally in the United States. Their family would hang around one place long enough for her dad to receive a paycheck, then they'd move on, always looking over their shoulder for the INS.

"Kayla, did you make the banner for the Hughes Bridal Shower?" Welcoming the intrusion, Kayla took a moment to gather her thoughts.

"Yes, actually, I did. It's in the top file drawer and is marked Hughes." Kayla backed up her entries from the morning's post. "Did you learn how to make the decorative wedding cake from bath linens?"

"Yes!" Alma exclaimed. "You pin the corners of four bath towels together then roll each one to the center and pin the rolls in place. Then do the same with four hand towels. The last layer is four washcloths, with intertwined beads and topped with silk flowers. It's very pretty."

Kayla smiled at a customer who entered, but carried on her conversation with Alma. "I thought it sounded like a unique idea. I still haven't found that *Hope Floats* music the bride's mother requested."

"Want me to order it online?"

"Oh, Alma, would you? Once the music arrives the preparations for the Hughes account will be complete."

"I'll take care of it right after lunch." Alma threw the bindings from another stack of helium balloons into the trash then approached the customer, her happy chatter confident and convincing.

"Kayla?"

"Hmm?" Lost in thought, Kayla hadn't heard Alma return.

"You seem to be feeling much better than last night. Have you decided what you're going to do about a place to stay?"

"I'm trying to figure it all out. I guess I'll rent an apartment."

"You know you're welcome to stay with me till you find something, right?"

"Yes, and I'm grateful you let me spend last night at your place, but we can't both live in a one-bedroom apartment. Tonight I'll get a motel room then take tomorrow morning off and look for a place."

Alma rang up and bagged the customer's purchases, while she discussed the theme in detail and threw in a few suggestions. When the customer left, Alma walked back to Kayla, a big grin on her face, eyebrows raised.

"What?" Kayla questioned.

"He's ba-ack."

Kayla glanced around Alma to see who was ba-ack.

"Oh, no, no, no, no," she wailed.

"Don't worry, Mama. It's all good." Alma borrowed Kayla's favorite line from a movie they'd gone to see recently.

Kayla rolled her eyes. "Ayi, Alma. You just don't get slang." She leaped from her chair and took off at a run toward the storeroom. "I'm not here," she called back over her shoulder.

"I'm not lying for you, Kayla Guerrero, so you march yourself right back out here."

With only her head sticking out around the storeroom door, Kayla explained, "I don't want you to lie. I just want you to be…creative."

Oh, why was he here again? She hadn't thought up a plan yet. He seemed the one most shook up over her mistake at the line shack. In a way, she liked that. He made her feel important by hanging on to every word she spoke. If she acted upset, he tried to calm her down. Last week, she'd booked a couple of evening parties. She'd arrived home late, only to open the door five minutes later to Marcelo delivering dinner. He'd even brought her tea to drink.

When she drove away from the line shack yesterday, she looked in her rearview mirror and saw him pitch a rock into the field, anger and frustration evident in the action. It would have been so easy to have stayed and let him take care of everything for her. Pride demanded that she leave, though. Yet his presence here, twice today, made it so much easier to swallow that pride. She felt… What was it she felt? Like maybe she had a little power over Marcelo. Was that a good thing? No matter what she'd told Alma that morning about Marc's just wanting her land, a part of her hoped she was wrong. A part that felt an awful lot like her heart.

Kayla had her hand on the knob, face pressed against

the door, listening for sounds from the other room. Nothing. The handle began to turn, and she jerked away from the door. She grabbed a box cutter and sliced into a package, folding back the top to reveal the contents.

"Hi, Kayla. Sorry to disturb you, but Alma told me to come on back."

I will dock her paycheck. "Hi, Mr. Fuentes. What brings you back so soon?"

"Kayla, if you call me Mr. Fuentes again, I'm going to—"

"You're going to what?" Kayla challenged him, curious as to his response. He studied each feature of her face intensely, lingering longest on her mouth.

"I'm going to kiss you," he answered, his voice low and smooth.

They stared at each other. Kayla's heart hammered foolishly. She heard the ticking of the clock that hung nearby. He murmured something and turned. Only then did she realize someone had knocked on the door and entered.

"Kayla, go to lunch. Heidi came in so you're free."

"Thanks, Alma. I'll grab a sub and come back here."

"No, Kayla. I'd like to buy you lunch." At her negative head shake, Marcelo held up a hand. "Please, we have a lot to talk about and I have a proposition for you."

Both Alma and Kayla stopped all forward movement. Kayla raised her eyebrows in question.

"Oh, this ought to be good," Alma muttered.

"It's nothing like that," Marcelo explained. "Kayla, I want you to move in to my place."

Momentarily speechless, she stared at him, stunned

by his suggestion. What astonished her even more was her response. She was so tempted by the idea.

Half in anticipation, half in dread she walked to the register and took her purse from the bottom drawer and walked out the door with Marcelo, leaving Alma with her mouth hanging open.

Chapter 8

They stopped at Keto's Café and ordered the lunch special. Kayla's stomach twisted and churned and she was afraid she'd be sick. They'd barely swallowed a few bites when Marcelo laid his fork down and took her hand. "Kayla, I'm sorry for not telling you the line shack was mine and I'm so sorry you were hurt, but once we started getting to know each other, I couldn't bear the thought of not seeing you or having you close by. Please say you'll forgive me. Please?"

Kayla stared into the face of the man in front of her. His firm mouth curled as if always on the verge of laughter, and that was what had drawn her to him. He found humor in almost everything and she needed that in her life. His dark hair magnified the inky blackness of his eyes. At the moment his brow was creased with worry. With the exception of her parents, she'd never had anyone even remotely care whether or not she was upset with them. It was a heady feeling.

"I forgive you, Marcelo. I'm the one who was in the wrong."

"Thanks." His voice grew husky and he lifted her hand to his lips.

She rested her chin on her other hand and smiled as she spoke teasingly. "And the proposition?"

"Ah, that." He chuckled. "That sure had Alma intrigued." He seemed lost in thought for a moment then cleared his throat, his fingers drawing patterns on the back of her hand.

Kayla felt a moment's apprehension. Alma wasn't the only one intrigued by his suggestion.

"My mother is back in town. She actually arrived in July, but then immediately went to Cancun with my aunt. Since then she's traveled a bit more. But now she's back at the house and has no plans for future travel until it's time to go back East. She gets lonely and bored at the hacienda and really needs something to occupy her time." He shook his head as if genuinely concerned. "If you move in it would solve both of our problems— you'd have a place to live and she would have someone to care for. She would cook and clean and possibly even help out at Confetti. Without pay, of course. She doesn't need money, just needs someone to mother. She needs something to do."

"I would love having her at Confetti. But she can be there without my moving into your house."

"But she'd feel like she was inviting herself to your

place. If you come to the house she will feel like she's helping you. That's important to my mom."

Kayla bent her head, letting her hair swing forward so that her face was partially hidden. She needed time to think this through. But time was something she didn't have. She hated staying in hotels; that had been a big part of life with her parents. She didn't have time to find an apartment, and a hotel would be her only choice tonight.

His fingers curved under her chin and he gently lifted her face to eye level. "Please don't hide your thoughts from me. Share them and let's work this out together."

"I have no other choice right now, so can I stay with you till I rent a place? Or is that not acceptable to you?"

"Perfectly okay." He threw money for their meal on the table and slid back his chair. She joined him and they walked to his truck hand in hand. He opened the driver-side door for her to climb into his truck, then stopped her from moving to the passenger seat, hooking her arm through his elbow as he turned the key.

She wondered what he was trying to say with his actions. That he loved her? When they were on the highway to Confetti, he took his right hand from the wheel and placed it over her hand.

"Can I ask you something that's lurked in the back of my mind since you arrived here?"

She nodded.

"What prompted you to move here when obviously you loved New York and planned to start your business there?"

Surprised by the question, she hesitated, torn by conflicting emotions.

"You don't have to answer if you don't want to."

"No, it's fine. I was just thrown for a moment." She felt an instant's squeezing hurt but started at the beginning and explained her childhood. "I hated our lifestyle—eighteen years of running, moving from city to city, dodging immigration officials. I never had a single birthday party, ever. Who would I invite? There was no time to make friends before we moved again. My parents thought it was an exciting lifestyle. Cocooned in their own little world, so in love, happily unaware that their only child needed stability and the familiar. I never once completed an entire year in the same school."

"That must have been hard." His voice was calm, his gaze steady.

"It was torture for a quiet, shy kid. College was my mainstay, though. Finally I could stay in one place, get to know people. I lived in the same dorm apartment, ate at an appointed time each day. My schedule was my best friend." She sighed. "Now I guess you know why having a home is so important to me."

She placed a hand against the deep, familiar pain in her chest. "But you know something? Despite eighteen years of being constantly uprooted, I loved my parents deeply. Some days I can still hear Mother's giggling complaints as Poppy whirled her round the kitchen, including a big kiss for their daughter, his day-old beard scratching my face." Tears threatened to choke her.

They pulled into the Confetti parking lot and he put the truck in Park. He pulled her into his arms and kissed her forehead. "Don't talk about it if you don't want to. I didn't mean to cause you pain."

She continued because now that she'd started, she wanted more than anything to share the rest of her story with him. "My parents came to my college graduation ceremonies. They were so proud, even more so when they presented me with a new car. I was driving the *gift* to a restaurant to celebrate, my parents following in their car, when a truck hit them head-on, killing them instantly. That scene will forever be etched in my memory. I sat in the emergency waiting room all alone, trying to deal with the loss, and life went on around me. There was no one to call, no one to come share the worst day of my life."

Marcelo rubbed her arm, comforting but waiting quietly for her to continue. He seemed to understand that she needed to get this out of her system. "A state trooper showed up with the personal belongings from their car. Going through the papers, I found a will and a life-insurance policy. I was the sole beneficiary. I contacted the lawyer. Even though my parents took equity from the insurance policy to buy the car, more than enough money was left to purchase stock for the store I'd planned and designed since I was eighteen.

"My mother had always said that they wanted to be buried in McAllen, where my mom had grown up. I chose a funeral home here. I didn't have a funeral. They had no immediate family and no close friends that I knew of.

"It finally sank in that I'd inherited my mom's family property, one hundred and twenty acres of ranch land with a small dwelling. I had a home, if I so chose. Which I did. I could put down roots and never move again."

She continued in a resigned voice. "I had the bodies flown from New York to Texas, passed through the legalities and laid them to rest in the *El Jardin Verde,* The Green Garden Cemetery." She remembered vividly the graveside event and was lost in thought for a few moments.

She came back to the present and continued her story. "The funeral home here in McAllen sent a pink limousine to transport me from the airport to the graveyard. Whoever heard of pink limousines for funerals? It looked like an advertisement for a makeup company."

Marcelo chuckled and she felt the rumble in his chest. How she'd come to be pressed close to his heart she didn't know, but it felt perfect. "I know the funeral home. It's been in business since before my grandparents died," he said.

She took a quick breath and continued. "On the plane back to New York I considered my options. My clothes, laptop and a few personal items were in the trunk of my car in New York. The rolled designs for Confetti were in a container on the backseat. That's all I had. There was nothing to tie me to New York or any other place. But here I had a home, and at the time it seemed like a good idea to make use of it.

"I had done a market analysis for New York, but I didn't see any reason why my plans wouldn't work just as well in McAllen. The plan, which I redesigned during my last year in college, was originally planned for busy, bustling Manhattan. A quick look at McAllen on the internet that same night showed it to be one of the fastest growing border towns along the Rio Grande, with well over a million people in residence, so my chances of success were exceptional—either in New York or Texas. I made the decision to relocate and I came to claim my inheritance. You know the story from there on."

"You've carried a heavy load all by yourself. I'm so proud of you. I wish I'd known all of this earlier, when you first arrived. You were grieving and I pestered you relentlessly."

"You did not. You were my salvation. I wallowed in despair but you kept showing up and your laughter and crazy sense of humor lifted my spirits." Becoming suddenly bold she lifted a hand and caressed his jaw. He turned his lips into her palm. He pushed a lone strand of hair from her cheek and turned her head as his descended for a kiss. She wondered briefly if a kiss could be spiritual because that's how she felt. As if her heart and soul were connected to this man.

He hugged her tightly then released her with a sigh. "We're about to be invaded by one curious Alma Cantu."

Kayla turned to the window facing Confetti and burst out laughing. Alma stood, hands on her hips, staring at them, then motioned for them to roll the window down.

"Are you all right?" She sounded like a mama bear ready to growl. "If you've hurt her, Marc Fuentes, you will answer to me. Understood?"

Kayla gave him a quick kiss then slid across to exit the passenger door. She closed the door, clasped Alma in a hug and walked her toward Confetti. Halfway there,

Alma balked and they skidded to a stop. "What's going on, Kayla Guerrero?"

Kayla watched the truck disappear out of sight and she couldn't stop the grin that turned into pure, joyous laughter. She twirled around, hands clutched together. "I think I'm in love."

Alma screamed and pulled her into a tight hug. "With Marc?"

"Well, of course with Marcelo. Who else would it be?"

"Just making sure. This is great news. He deserves a good woman like you."

"I just spilled my guts to him completely, and he listened and sympathized. How many other men would do that? He's so sweet and thoughtful."

Kayla expelled a long sigh of contentment. She sure hoped she deserved a good man like Marcelo. She felt a newly awakened sense of life. Tragedy had etched its mark on her but her tears were now gone, evaporated by an indefinable feeling of rightness.

Kayla had been in Marcelo's hacienda for two weeks now and felt at home with Marta fussing over her. It was almost like having a mother again. She especially liked the evenings when the entire family got together. Like now. She loved hearing the brothers tease, threaten and try to top each other's jokes. She shared understanding looks with Carina and Marta. These guys were the cream of the crop. They cared for each other, and their attention to the women in their lives was wonderful to see. She'd caught Marc's brothers checking her out several times and she'd seen Marcelo's threatening look. It was all she could do not to laugh out loud. Raoul, the youngest, seemed to dare Marcelo to do something about it till Juan Antonio chucked him on the shoulder.

"You own Confetti? I was next door the day the sign went up." Raoul had singled her out in the kitchen. "Unique design."

"Thanks. I'm pretty satisfied with how they painted it."

"And how is business going?"

"Really good. Beyond what I even dreamed." Kayla wondered briefly if the younger Fuentes man was a player, a flirt who said all the right things to many different girls. Did he even know that Adele was head over heels in love with him?

Carina strolled into the kitchen and Kayla breathed a sigh of relief. "Raoul, where's Adele? Why didn't she come with you?"

He pushed away from the island counter and straightened, sarcasm dripping from his voice. "How should I know? And I didn't ask her to come with me. Why would I want to ruin an evening with my family?"

Carina raised a dismissive hand, apparently unconcerned that Raoul appeared upset. "My bad. I thought this might be an evening when she was on your good side. Don't get your shorts in a wad."

Kayla bit her lip to keep from cracking up. She'd never heard the lovely Carina be anything other than nice, and her comments ranked on the side of insolent. Her eyes widened in surprise when Raoul grabbed her in a wrestler hold and rubbed her head with his fist.

Carina screamed for Tonio and began pinching Raoul's stomach. They were dodging around the kitchen and Kayla moved swiftly out of their way. Raoul screamed like a girl when Carina finally got hold of his underarm and pinched for dear life. He let her go right as Juan Antonio and Marcelo sauntered into the room.

"Are you messing with my girl again, baby brother?" Juan Antonio lightly popped the back of his head. Marcelo grabbed Raoul from behind, pinning his arms to his side, allowing Carina to swoop in for another pinch on his stomach. She had a hard time since he struggled fiercely with his brother. She finally gave up, running for cover in Juan Antonio's arms when Marcelo let Raoul loose. The evil glint in Carina's eyes belied the huge grin on her face and Kayla finally laughed.

So the pretty lady didn't take mouthing off from one of the Fuentes brothers. Interesting. And it had been her way of taking up for Adele. Maybe Adele was right and Raoul needed to grow up. But he'd shown adult acceptance of Carina giving him tit for tat; well, if you didn't count the horseplay.

When Carina produced a movie about Queen Esther, all three men groaned, but Kayla watched as Juan Antonio settled his fiancée beside him on the love seat, leaving almost the entire second seat available. Kayla sat on the sofa between Raoul and Marcelo but was afraid to lean against Marcelo the way Carina did with Juan Antonio. The decision was taken from her, though, when Marcelo laid his head in her lap and propped his legs over the end of the sofa, preparing to fall asleep.

Raoul, who'd slyly placed his hand on the seat behind

her, drew back in surprise and immediately dropped his hand. "I'm outta here." He stood and walked to the door slapping it open with the flat of his hand.

"Good idea, bro, cause I'd hate to have to break that arm you started to place around my girl." Marcelo's voice was full of humor but held an underlying threat. The door shut with a bang and Marta came out of her bedroom to see the cause of such noise. She followed Raoul out onto the veranda and they saw her sit in one of the rocking chairs where Raoul joined her.

Kayla looked at the other occupants in the room and could have crawled under the sofa. Carina, frozen in place, still held the remote pointed at the TV. Juan Antonio reached over and high-fived Marcelo. "Well done, Marco Polo, well done."

Carina pressed the play button and the film began scrolling the actors' names. When everyone appeared interested in the movie Kayla glanced down at Marcelo and did a thorough study of his features. She gently ran her hand through his hair and with her other hand she traced his eyebrows then his lips and cupped his jaw. He was the most beautiful man she'd ever seen. Bits and pieces of the movie filtered in and she became engrossed in the story of Esther and how she went before the king. Her hand still cupped Marcelo's jaw, her other absentmindedly stroking his hair.

When the king kissed Esther, she looked at Marcelo's lips and let her thumb lightly touch them. So engrossed was she in discovering the extent of her feelings for him, her heart jolted when she saw his eyes were open and his gaze, soft as a caress, traveled over her face and searched her eyes.

She laid her head back against the sofa cushions. Unsuccessfully she tried to throttle the dizzying emotions racing through her. She had dreamed of a love like this. She'd asked the Lord for someone who wasn't ashamed to say grace or read his Bible in front of her. It was evident he loved his mother and his brothers; that was another plus. His character was one she could admire and his laughter lit a smoldering flame of joy inside her. She wanted to cherish tonight, to hug it to her heart. Just like Esther and Ruth in the Bible, she'd waited till God sent the other half of her whole.

The movie ended and Marcelo sat up while Carina and Juan Antonio removed the DVD and turned off the player. He stood, and taking her hands, pulled her up. But he kept his distance and continued to do so as they went out onto the veranda and said goodbye to his brothers and Carina.

Finally he put an arm around Kayla's shoulder and when his mother went into the house he whispered into her hair, "I have a gift for you in the truck. Walk with me."

She placed an arm about his waist but at his unresponsiveness she remained silent and contemplative. He lifted a basket from the truck seat and handed it to her.

Kayla stared at the basket packed full of bath and body products, all feminine and pretty. A large candle sat near the top and she saw several of her personal favorites. Tears formed in her eyes at the sweetness of the gift.

"Hey, hey. What's this?" With his thumb Marcelo caught a lone tear before it could travel down her cheek.

He had no way of knowing that she'd never received a gift from anyone other than her parents and those had been few and far between. She said the first thing that came to her mind.

"I thought you were upset at me for being so forward tonight." She sniffed the package from the outside. "I couldn't seem to stop. I wanted to commit your face to memory. Does that make sense?"

"Perfect." He kissed her forehead. "I'll send you a text tonight. Read it and understand, okay?"

Kayla noticed the teasing laughter was back in his eyes. She laughed gently. They walked back to the house hand in hand, and at the door they parted with nothing more than a whispered good-night and a lingering handclasp.

When the phone dinged an incoming text message, she pressed the letter icon on her phone with all the eagerness of a kid on Christmas morning.

Perfect night, my love. Intense. My fault. Should not have put you in that position. Made purity commitment in teens, plan to keep. Wow! You knock my socks off. I'll guard us better from now on. Deal?

How could she not agree when she felt exactly the same way? She realized now how easy it could be to sin. Her emotions had been all over the place. Zooming at her like a race car on the track. But her man planned to protect her and keep her out of trouble. He wouldn't tell her if she loved him she'd do whatever he asked. In other words, he offered protection and respect. If possible, that made her love for him even stronger. She'd be lying, though, if she didn't admit that a part of her reveled in the ability to have this kind of power over him. But as in the story of Queen Esther, power should be tempered with patience and God's timing.

She texted back:

Deal! I place myself into your very capable hands. Take good care of me. I will cherish your words. There are no shadows in my heart tonight, just pure joy. Night, Marco Polo. Lol.

Chapter 9

"Miss Guerrero, would you like to offer your thoughts on what's been the major change in your life since you've been an adult?"

Butterflies fluttered in Kayla's stomach and slightly elevated heartbeats pulsed in the vein along her neck. She'd never been good at speaking in public and though this was just a Sunday School class, the result was the same.

Marcelo shifted on the seat beside her. Was he nervous for her? They'd gone around the room and everyone had contributed to the discussion. Now it was her turn. When Marcelo had spoken he'd been humorous and completely at ease. She didn't have that talent but she could stand on her own.

"Moving to Texas was a huge change, but opening

my business, Confetti, made me take risks I'd never taken before."

"And have the risks been worth it so far?"

"Oh, yes. Beyond my wildest dreams." The exuberance in her voice made her classmates laugh.

"I know I'm putting you on the spot but you're a fresh new voice among us so if you wouldn't mind, could you elaborate on the risks you've taken? That really would help explain our lesson theme today."

Kayla minded all right, but asked so nicely, how could she refuse? She still wasn't used to baring her soul in Sunday School like the lifetime churchgoers seemed to be. Putting it all out there felt like a bigger risk than opening a new business.

"Oddly, the greatest risks have been following the rules. The government mandates are so rigid and sometimes the opportunity arises where you have the choice to be honest or let small things you think are ridiculous slide. But if you do, then most often you end up backtracking or doing something over or extending the inspections. In the long run, it's better to do things right and not take unnecessary risks."

"Are there situations when it's worth it to take some risks?"

Kayla thought for a moment. "We have better resources, more knowledge and teaching aids today than ever before so we actually can be prepared for the government regulations and not be tempted to take risks in that area. But when someone is vague on the type of decorations they want for a party, for example, or they don't thoroughly explain what they want and we can't reach them for more information, then we choose what we think is right. Sometime it works and sometimes it doesn't. It's a risk we must take."

"Thank you, Miss Guerrero. That is exactly how the risk takers in the Old Testament handled things. Moses, Abraham, they took risks and weren't afraid to walk by faith."

The teacher continued on with the lesson. Kayla breathed a sigh of relief. Why was she putting herself through this? Because Sunday School was important to Marcelo. They'd talked throughout the past week about what they wanted from each other and faithful church attendance was important to him. By that he meant Sunday morning—both Sunday School and worship service—Sunday night and Wednesday prayer meeting. It was all new to Kayla. She'd gone a few times a year when she was in college but had never committed to more than that. But she was so glad Marcelo had shown her his heart on this subject. Talking over spiritual things in the evenings had bonded them in ways she only dreamed of. They did nightly devotions with his mother and when he had his Bible on his lap as he did now, he appeared more handsome, more attractive than ever before.

She knew what Alma meant when she said she wanted to marry a preacher; that a man of God was passionate, a leader, had appealing qualities every woman desired. That's how she felt when Marcelo shared his thoughts on God's words. Like the Scripture said, her heart safely trusted in him.

The buzzer rang, ending the class.

"Miss Guerrero?"

What now? Did he plan after-class detention for her? Kayla paused at the door. The last person filed past. Marcelo remained at her side.

"Thank you so much for participating this morning. I unashamedly used you to make a very important point. Everyone always listens to a new voice, especially one so successful early on in their life. For this age group, risk taking should be carefully guided by the Word of God. You'll be a very welcome addition to our class. I look forward to getting to know you better." He shook Kayla's hand.

"Marcelo. Good to see you, man."

Kayla left the room with a deep sense of satisfaction she'd not felt in a long time. She was learning that when she included God in decisions and when she gave of herself to help others, she felt complete. Whole. The void inside her grew little and good things and feelings filled her up.

"Excuse me?" Marcelo's voice intruded on her thoughts. "Earth to Kayla."

"I'm sorry. What did you say?" They were sitting in the sanctuary waiting on the preaching service to start. Kayla loved this part of the day. Pastor Scott had a marvelous and inventive way of explaining the Scriptures.

"Lunch? Where are we going?"

"You're always hungry, Marcelo. You just had breakfast a little over an hour ago." She giggled as he bumped shoulders in a threatening tease.

"I'm a growing boy. I need protein."

She looked at the man beside her and her heart skipped a few beats. "No."

"No?" He eyed her inquisitively, an occasional approving glance at her lips.

"You're definitely not a boy." They exchanged a subtle look of amusement.

"Watch it, Miss Guerrero." He used the same inflection as the Sunday School teacher. "You're in church."

She smiled at him with tender wonder; how had she been so lucky to gain the love of this handsome man? Her reaction to his teasing comment seemed to amuse him. He pulled her hand through his arm as the choir began to file in. She leaned over and whispered in his ear the name of his favorite restaurant. He tilted his head so he could hear her better and just the smell of him caused shivers of awareness.

None of your highfalutin business. Can I say that and not get kicked out? Years of training held his tongue. They were waiting for a table at the restaurant, seated on a bench that wrapped around the waiting area and the winter Texan beside him kept asking him personal questions. All Marcelo wanted was to have one-on-one time with Kayla and here he was engaged in conversation with a total stranger about the benefits of raising grass-fed beef.

"I'm meeting friends here in a bit. Thought I'd come ahead and reserve the table. This is a good place to eat and the wait is always worth it."

Marcelo nodded.

"Where is your ranch located, if you don't mind my

asking?" Marcelo gave directions and wondered briefly if the man was a crook intent on breaking and entering or possibly even a cattle thief. He remained a little vague in the exact location of his place.

Their names were called at the same time and the stranger walked side by side with them till they were separated by the table arrangements. He pulled a card from his pocket and handed it to Marcelo. "Call me sometime." *Why,* Marcelo thought sourly. *So you can torture me more?*

Finally seated and order placed, he reached across the table for Kayla's hands. He wished they'd been seated in a booth so she could sit close to him. He was a goner. He hated being away from her for any length of time. When she left for work in the mornings, he counted the hours till she returned in the evenings. J.T. called it nauseating.

"Look, Marcelo. Is that not the cutest thing?" Kayla nodded in the direction of a nearby table where a boy about three years old fed pieces of fries to his little brother who looked about two.

"You like children?"

"I love children." She flirted with him. "I plan to have a dozen or so."

"Oh, you do, do you? And how do you plan to feed your large brood?"

"Not hard to figure that one out. I have a friend who owns a cattle ranch. I'll buy a few chickens for eggs and we're set."

"Think that'll work, huh?"

"Oh, yes. Works for him. He thinks vegetables are

mortal enemies, so a slab of meat a day should make those young'uns fat and sassy."

Kayla was surprised when his brows drew together in an affronted frown. He let her hands go so the waiter could set their plates in front of them. As soon as the waiter left, Kayla asked nervously, "You're upset?" She wouldn't hurt his feelings for anything in the world, but come on, he teased all the time. If he couldn't take it he shouldn't dish it out.

"Let's pray." He bowed his head and began the blessing over the food. Kayla sat there, blank, amazed and very shaken with her eyes wide-open. "Father, thank You for this food we are about to eat, especially the baked potato from the vegetable family, the corn, also a vegetable and help it to nourish our bodies. Teach Kayla that she should close her eyes when prayers are being offered and that if she can't take it she shouldn't dish it out. In Jesus's name, oh, and Lord, You might want to warn her that You can't con a con. Amen."

Despite her angst, Kayla burst out laughing and hit him with her napkin-rolled utensils. "That was pathetic. Now say a real blessing." He took her hand and blessed the food correctly.

Kayla had chosen a cup of soup and a sandwich. She offered Marcelo a bite, amazed at the thrill it gave her when his mouth closed over the same spoon she'd used. Was this why her mother followed her dad all over the United States, never settling in one place? Because suddenly she understood more clearly the difficulty in parting from someone you loved.

The winter Texan stopped by their table and asked for Marcelo's number.

Kayla stared at the man. What was happening in the world today? Had everyone taken a manners hiatus? She switched her gaze to the soup in front of her.

The man left and Marcelo seemed upset but determined to forget the intrusion.

"About the dozen kids you want? Is that true?"

Kayla thought about teasing again but he looked serious so she answered truthfully. "Not an exact dozen but at least four."

"Seriously?"

She nodded. "You don't want children?" Kayla hoped her smile was noncommittal. The last thing she wanted to do was scare him away.

"You sold me on the dozen but I can settle for four. I think five would be a better number, though. That way when there's a disagreement the majority will rule." The mischievous glint in his eyes warned Kayla that he might instigate a lot of those said disagreements. She chuckled.

"And what if all five are girls?"

Marcelo paused midbite, a look of horror on his face. Kayla put her napkin over her mouth to stifle the giggles.

"Then it's back to the dozen." He calmly began to chew again.

Kayla couldn't control her burst of laughter.

"I love being with you, Marcelo." Her words caused his expressive face to become almost somber. "You bring such joy to my life. I've never been so happy."

"I feel the same, sweetheart." He reached for her hand. "When you say things like that, I feel powerful, like I'm the strongest man on the earth." He raised her hand to his lips.

When they had finished eating he laid money on the table and slid from the booth, offering his hand to help her up. "Let's get out of here."

He stole kisses all the way to the truck then hooked her arm through his as he drove away. She laid her head on his shoulder, peace strumming through her and a feeling that she was in God's perfect will.

"Kayla, I want to know everything about you."

Lulled by her quiet thoughts it took Kayla a moment to respond. "Mmm-hmm, ask me anything."

He chuckled, but she knew it pleased him because he hugged her arm closer to his side. "You've told me you moved a lot. What kind of schools did you go to?"

She had no clue what he was talking about. She raised her head from his shoulder and tentatively asked. "What do you mean?"

"Did you attend public school, Christian school or some other private school?"

"I always went to public school. What about you?"

"Public school. And I got in a lot of trouble in high school due to peer pressure."

"I was never at one school long enough to experience peer pressure."

"For real?"

"Every time I got close to someone and thought I finally would have a close friend, we moved. New school.

New people. I hated it." Kayla could hear the bitterness in her words.

"And we never moved. Same people every year in school. Half my teachers had spouses who worked for my Gramps." He was quiet for a while. "We have very different backgrounds, but that's not a bad thing, is it? The Lord has blessed us abundantly, Kayla."

She laid her head back on his shoulder, trying not to be so affected by his words. At the base of her throat a pulse beat and swelled as though her heart had risen from its usual place. This man had become as important to her survival as breathing. "You see the good in everything, Marcelo. You inspire me to do better."

He kissed the top of her head and she knew he felt the same emotional charge.

"I love you, Kayla Guerrero."

Marcelo ran a hand through his hair. He'd come so close to blowing it. God had sent the answer to his prayers. He stared at the business card in amazement. The Bar-S-Ranch, Mike Whittington, Owner. The biggest cattle operation in Wyoming. And they wanted him to supply them with grass-fed beef. A large advance to cover expenses and bulk payment upon delivery. His house would be paid for by the first of the year.

He took out his cell to call Kayla and share the news. She answered immediately.

"Hi, babe. What's up?" Her cheerful voice never failed to move him.

"Remember the man who kept interrupting us last Sunday at the restaurant?"

"Yeah."

Marcelo explained who he was and what he wanted. "Can you believe that? The price of one delivery will pay the house off and I'll be debt free. At my age." He could hear the excitement in his voice.

"Wow, that's great. I'm so happy for you."

"For us, Kayla, for us."

"Thanks for that. I needed to hear it today. And I'm so proud of your hard work. You deserve good things happening to you. Why don't you come to town and have lunch with me? We'll celebrate."

"What? You don't have a lunch partner again?"

She laughed infectiously. "You know me so well. Actually, not just because I hate eating alone but that soup your mom sent with me is enough to feed an army. And this way, we can celebrate and I'll have the pleasure of your company during the meal."

"I'm like, totally shocked that you'd want my company."

She laughed at his mockery of Heidi, one of her part-time workers, a teenager who used the word *like* to an irritating degree.

"Yes, well, if you're going to misbehave you'd better stay at home. I'll get the guy cleaning the parking lot to eat with me."

"What?" Kayla could hear the surprise in his voice. She'd never teased him in this manner and was surprised at how low she suddenly felt. "Ouch, that hurt."

"Oh, and I didn't like it, either. I apologize, my darling. I would never do that to you. It makes me sick to my stomach just to think about it. We should never joke about things like that."

"Apology accepted."

"Thanks. So will you come have lunch with me and let me make it up to you?"

"Just try and stop me."

"What can I do for you this morning, Marcelo?"

Marcelo heaved a sigh as he climbed into the barber's chair, aggravated that he had to get a professional haircut instead of the usual one Flipper gave him. But per his mother, with the wedding planning, showers, bachelor parties and on and on, there would be endless pictures taken and his hair would need to be styled. Unaccustomed to professional hair styling, he decided to check out different, and to his way of thinking, most absurd looks till he found one that suited. If he started now, maybe he would be decided on which haircut looked best on him for the wedding of the year. If they messed it up this time he would know what to do to fix it a few days before the wedding. If he waited, in the family pictures he would look like a geek. He knew all this because his mother had spent the better part of the morning nagging him.

"Need a styled haircut, Sam."

"Any ideas?"

"Not a one. I like it as it is but Mom says it needs to be styled for the wedding." He wasn't going to tell anyone because the plans weren't finalized in his mind just yet, but there might be another occasion for him to look tall, dark and handsome.

"Okay. Wanna shave, too? You're looking pretty scruffy." Sam Gonzales had been his dad's friend and had cut J.T. and Raoul's hair since they were boys but Marcelo never ventured far from the ranch and Flipper's cuts suited him fine.

"Sure. Might as well get the works." Marcelo leaned his head back and closed his eyes as Sam placed a warm, moist cloth across the lower half of his face. With any luck, Sam wouldn't talk and he could examine the insides of his eyelids for holes. A few more minutes of sleep might clear the fog from his brain.

As the warmth seeped into his skin, he became preoccupied with thoughts of a most satisfying nature. Kayla Guerrero sharing lunch with him, smiling at him, one moment serious, the next teasing, her small hand clasped in his. Her hair smelled of honeysuckle and appeared to have a blond thread filtering through the brown tresses. Kayla gave an impression of unusual strength and suppleness, and acted as spirited as an untamed horse. She challenged him. He'd had a pretty cool childhood, and she'd suffered. Did she whine about it? No. She owned a successful store and had made it a specialty place by adding catering and candy making.

He loved when they talked about plans for the future. He wasn't sure she was even aware of how serious that made their relationship. Her closeness and the spontaneous compliments she paid him had taken his breath away.

"Marcelo, did you hear me?"

He heard the impatience in Sam's voice. "Sorry, Sam, I was miles away. What did you say?"

"I said, 'stretch your head back so I can reach your neck more easily.'"

Marcelo complied and sat immobile as the razor scraped over his chin.

"Got your mind on a pretty little *señorita* this morning?" Sam wiped the razor on a towel, then paused, allowing Marcelo time to answer. This familiarity with a person's private affairs drove Raoul crazy, but Marcelo sorta liked it. It made him feel like part of a big family. He accepted it in the spirit intended, as genuine interest and caring.

"Matter of fact, Sam, you hit the nail on the head," Marcelo admitted unashamedly. "How do you get a woman you're interested in to marry you?"

"Do like I did with my Norma. We had a tamale-making day over on the Rio Grande and I caught her behind the barn and gave her a big smooch. Was no doubt in her mind after that."

"She liked that, did she?"

"Oh, no. She hauled off and slapped me a good 'un. Wouldn't speak to me for weeks. Said I'd tarnished her reputation."

"Then how'd you get her to forgive you?" Marcelo leaned back again as Sam approached. Maybe there would be a nugget in this story he could use on Kayla.

"I asked her to marry me."

Marcelo sat up suddenly, the razor nicking the edge of his chin.

"Watch out there, boy. Wouldn't want to cut your throat or anything." Sam's voice held both humor and a warning.

"You had to offer marriage to get her to talk to you?" Disbelief caused his voice to rise, so Marcelo swallowed and relaxed against the seat. "That sounds like you were coerced into marrying Miss Norma."

"If *coerced* means held at gunpoint, well, no, I wasn't. But if it means I had no choice, then, yep, I was coerced." Sam blotted the small trickle of blood from Marcelo's chin, his hearty chuckle floating up from his throat.

Marcelo sat stock-still. This conversation was *not* garnering the information he needed. "Sam, if I didn't know better, I'd say you'd been hitting the bottle. Stop talking in double entendres."

"Double what? Me? Son, you're not even speaking the English language."

"Sam, why'd you feel you had to marry Miss Norma if her dad wasn't holding a shotgun on you?" Laughter filled Marcelo's voice, and he began to wish he'd never started this discussion.

"Well, it got to the point I couldn't eat, sleep or think of anything else but her. I wanted to be in her presence every minute of the day, even if she was mad at me. I needed her to keep me sane. I still like to get her riled up so we can hug and smooch a little bit, and make things right again."

Suddenly his dad's old friend made perfect sense.

Chapter 10

Finally, Kayla surveyed the church fellowship hall with a sense of accomplishment and pride. The flowers and decorations for Carina's bridal shower complemented Confetti's chocolates perfectly. The cake server and knife looked majorly expensive and the cake could not have turned out better. Everything had fallen right into place. Once they unpacked the silverware and cutlery she and Alma could enjoy the rest of the evening. Heidi and Josh were on duty to serve, and a crew had been hired to clean up.

Since the wedding would garner major fanfare, Carina had chosen to have the main bridal shower just shy of two months before the wedding. She stated emphatically that she had no desire to wind up exhausted the day of the wedding. Kayla loved this because it also gave her added time to perfect the arrangements. And according to Carina's planner, with all the individual parties, private showers, even teas scheduled for the wedding, it served everyone's purpose to divide time between the two main events.

"Hey, you can stop watching the clock now. It's quarter to six." Alma grinned, raised her arms above her head, stretching from side to side to straighten the kinks from her shoulders.

"What are you talking about, woman?" Kayla guessed what Alma teased about but played innocent.

"You've been glancing at that clock for an hour now. Marcelo just pulled up outside."

"I could have been making sure we were set up on time." She wasn't going to lie. She had been waiting to see him all day.

Alma laughed. "Right, and I'm the one this party is for. Give it up, girl, and go get your man."

"You know, I think I'll do just that." She took off her apron, folded it and put it on one of the clean serving plates, then carried it through to the kitchen. "You coming with me to greet the guests?" Kayla, Marcelo, Raoul, Adele, Alma and a missionary friend of Juan Antonio's, Rick Garrett, were the actual wedding party and were to greet the guests, seat them and serve at Carina's bridal shower that was given by the church.

"The rest of the food might arrive while we're gone. I'd better stay put in case it does." There were several food items that Kayla and Alma couldn't make, tamales being the most difficult.

"Josh and Heidi can handle it. Let's go so you won't miss out on anything."

Alma complied and they arrived at the same time as Marcelo, Raoul and Adele.

Kayla accepted Marcelo's discreet kiss and whispered to him, "I have so much to tell you."

"Yeah? Me, too."

"I can hardly wait." She stood in the crook of his arm, taking a few moments to enjoy her man. And he seemed to share the same idea.

"Wish we were home already." He barely raised his voice above a whisper, but she heard him and touched his chest in an instinctive gesture of comfort.

"You are so handsome in a suit." She straightened his tie, her back to the crowd, and he used the cover to steal another quick kiss.

"All right, you two. Behave or I'll make you come sit by me." Marta swatted his arm as she passed. He grabbed her and kissed her cheek. Her gentle laugh rippled through the air. An expression of delight filled her eyes. "I love you, son, but you're up to something. I'm your mother. I know all the signs."

"What? Can't a son kiss his mother without being accused of mischief?"

"Not my sons. And you three had better not start a ruckus tonight." When he rolled his eyes, she swatted him again. "I mean it, Marcelo. You boys are getting too old for horseplay. You'd better remember who gave you life and who can—"

"Take it away. Got it, Mom."

Kayla couldn't help herself; she burst out laughing. Marcelo looked like a little boy caught with his hand in the cookie jar.

At that moment, the fellowship hall began to fill with people. The Fuentes family was known by people from one end of the valley to the other. Everyone began to do the jobs assigned them. Each couple escorted guests to tables decorated by Confetti. Kayla had never felt more successful than she did tonight. Her business was catering one of the biggest social events of the season. She and Alma had made the decorations and prepared the food. She wished her parents could see her now. At times like this she missed them more than ever.

She had become separated from Marcelo at some point during the evening, but suddenly he was in front of her, regarding her with somber curiosity. "What's wrong?"

How she loved this man who recognized her emotions. "How could anything be wrong on a perfect night like tonight?"

"And yet I see sadness in those lovely eyes. So tell me, sweetheart, or I'll have to kidnap you and kiss it out of you." His gentle teasing did the trick and she felt the corners of her mouth tip up.

"Not a very menacing threat, Marco Polo. I think I'll keep my secret."

He feigned picking her up in his arms and she pushed him away. Laughing, she threatened to tell his mother. He winced.

"I love how you love me." Kayla sought for words to say just what she meant. "I know I say it often but it's precious to me, this love. It's so amazing what we feel for each other."

"It's incredible, but please tell me what has upset

you. Allow me to fix it." His arm slid around her waist and she curled into the curve of his body.

"There's nothing to fix. I thought how much I'd love for my parents to see this tonight. They would be so proud of their baby girl."

"Yes they would, *mi amor*. And I'm sorry they're not here for you." Softly his breath fanned her face as he turned so he could look her in the eye. "But I'm here for you and will do my best to honor your special days and cheer you on."

They ate together and shared a table with Marcelo's mother, Raoul, Adele and Adele's dad. Juan Antonio, Carina, Rick Garrett and his wife, Marsha, were seated with Carina's mother and two brothers.

When the meal was over, everyone lingered over the fellowship and cake. Then a mariachi band played and sang traditional Spanish love songs. Kayla felt pride in her heritage. One thing was for certain, the Hispanic race knew how to throw a good party.

Before Kayla entered his life, loneliness had become Marcelo's permanent companion. He possessed a friendly personality that drew people to him, but he had reached a point in his life where he wanted more. He had yearned for a home, a place of his own. Then his mother had deeded the ranch land to him. He'd worked from sunup to sunset for four long years, building his stock and installing irrigation systems. He'd bought a truck and a cattle hauler then finally gotten a loan and built his house. But none of that had been as satisfying as it was now, sharing it with Kayla. His heart told him he'd found his other half—his soul mate. Right here in Hidalgo County where he'd been born and raised. God had brought her to him. And with that realization, he set a plan in motion. A fancy bridal shower and wedding would not be the only romantic celebration in the Fuentes family. Oh, no. There would be one more party. He just had to set things in motion.

Marcelo rubbed his hands briskly. It was a little chilly outside; temperatures sat at seventy-three degrees. But the weather had afforded them a reprieve from the hundred and six temperatures of last month so seventy-three felt cool.

He loved it when a plan came together. And he'd been planning for weeks. Today was the day. Kayla would finally have a party and she didn't even realize she had planned it herself. He'd made a call to a friend and had her ask Kayla to use her own imagination and favorite colors to design an engagement party. Kayla thought she was doing it for his friend. She'd completed the last Confetti balloon yesterday and the lady had picked up all the decorations and at this very moment was placing them all through his house.

He checked the dresser drawer for the umpteenth time. The vintage antique-style, radiant-cut diamond ring was still there. Alma would escort her home, blindfolded, and remove it when she entered his house. Hopefully soon to be their house. He would ask for her hand in marriage, but because she'd never had a party on any of her special days, he intended this to be a first of many in their lives together.

The lawn was decorated in small glowing lights;

soft and slow music played from speakers placed un-
obtrusively around the backyard. All was set. Now if
she would just say yes. He had no reason to think she
wouldn't, but with women, one never knew.

Forty minutes later the crowd had arrived in full
force. Apparently clued in to his nervousness, they mingled quietly with one another, offering various forms of
pity or congratulations. Then she was there. Stunningly
beautiful, she took his breath away. Alma removed the
blindfold and Kayla glanced around uncertainly. Her
beautiful eyes took in their many friends and family
members, and the decorations covering almost every
spot of available space.

She'd made flowers of tulle and placed tiny white
lights within the folds of the sheer cloth, making it glow.
Candles were lit in various places and the smell wafted
over the rooms, pleasing the senses. Then those honey-
gold eyes sought and found him.

He walked to her, took her hand and led her to the
middle of the living room. The people granted them
walking space but quickly closed in, forming a complete circle.

He faced her and took both hands in his. Leaning
forward, he whispered in her ear. "You take my breath
away, Kayla. I love you so much."

She glanced nervously at the people surrounding
them. "What's going on?"

He cleared his throat and spoke loudly enough for
everyone present to hear. "Kayla Guerrero, you rode
into my life in a dust storm and stole my line shack.
If that wasn't devious enough, you stole my heart and

I never want it back. I give it to you for safekeeping. I love you with my whole being and I can't imagine life without you." He went down on one knee, one of her hands still clasped in his. He held out the ring. "Will you marry me?"

The tears swelled up then tipped over and ran down her beautiful face, but he didn't mind. Her head nodded and he stood and gathered her tightly in his arms. His own eyes suspiciously damp, he kissed her hungrily, tasting the saltiness he wasn't sure was his or hers. He became aware of the applause of the guests and drawing back a bit, took her hand in his and slid the ring onto her finger. She held it up to see then clasped it to her chest. "It's beautiful. I love it." Placing her arms around his shoulders, she buried her face against his throat. A slow rendition of "Amazing Grace" came through the speakers and the crowd quieted. He danced her gently around the small space and her breath fanned his face. How could this not be considered a spiritual thing since he felt God's blessings oh so abundantly on their engagement?

Kayla abandoned herself to the whirl of sensation invading even the pores of her skin. Her heart felt likely to explode. So many friends were there to wish them well, and the house competed with Confetti for happiness decorations. And Marcelo? Oh, my soul, she could not take her eyes off him. She leaned back in his arms and his lips parted in a dazzling display of straight, white teeth. His black hair gleamed in the lights, but those eyes. Ah, she went weak at the knees. His eyes burned with promises that beckoned to her irresistibly.

"How are you doing, my love?"

"I'd like to tell everyone something. Can you stop the music?"

In less than a minute those assembled waited quietly for Kayla to speak. She swallowed nervously then looked at the floor for a moment, gathering her thoughts.

"I'm not sure my sweet Marcelo knows what a perfectly splendid thing he has accomplished here tonight so I want to share my thoughts with all of you. I've never had a party in my life." She smiled at the gasps from several guests. "I've had cake and ice cream with my parents for birthdays but that's all. But never once have I had any friends or other family members in attendance. This—" her arm swept slowly to encompass the room and the overhead decorations "—is beyond my wildest dreams. To share it with all my friends is icing on the cake. You look so beautiful and whoever did the decorations, well, you're hired at Confetti." The room erupted in laughter, surprising her. Marcelo explained that she, Kayla, had made the decorations for Carina's mother. Carina's mother, with help from Alma, had willingly carried out the cover-up once she'd learned the reason for it.

Marcelo drew her close as if he couldn't stand to be parted from her. But she pushed gently against him and continued her speech. "Then, as this is my party and I did the work for it, let me just take a few moments more of your time and then the best food you'll ever taste will be served." She took Marcelo's hand in both of hers and silence fell on the group. She directed her next words to him. "My darling Marcelo. That you would even understand what it would mean to do this for me assures me that you know my heart intimately. When God gave you to me, He filled all the missed holidays and special times in my life. I feel whole, complete and blessed beyond measure to be your fiancée. The day doesn't begin till I hear your voice and the sun doesn't dare shine till I see your face. I love you to eternity and back."

She saw the tenderness of his gaze and raised his hand to her lips. She kissed the back of his hand and then the palm. By then the crowd was in full accord calling, *"beso, beso."* Kayla felt happy to oblige. She drew his face to hers and quickly kissed him, barely a breath of a touch. She raised one eyebrow in challenge and turned away but he was having none of it. With one arm behind her shoulders and the other in front holding her, he bent her backward and planted a tantalizing kiss that left her in no doubt of his feelings.

The crowd cheered but followed the voice of someone inviting them for food out in the courtyard. Left to their privacy, Kayla knew she'd always cherish the moments in their lives when they were totally alone. "I can't wait to call myself Kayla Fuentes." She admired the ring on her finger. "Oh, honey, we will have such a perfect life."

"Not too perfect, I hope." He nuzzled the curve of her neck, his breath warm and moist against her face. "We need to fight so we can make up."

She settled back, enjoying the feel of his arms around

her. It would be hard to top this evening. "Thank You, Lord."

As if on the same wavelength, Marcelo echoed, "Yes, Lord, we humbly thank You."

The next day Kayla walked around in a daze. She looked at the ring on her finger several times an hour. She belonged to Marcelo. He loved her. Alma came into the storeroom and talked over a few business matters with Kayla. She finally stood to leave, shaking her head and muttering about Kayla's mind being in the clouds, apparently unaware how Kayla's feet no longer touched the ground, either. Kayla heard Alma saying goodbye to some customers through the fog in her brain. Could she fall more in love? She didn't think so. She was a hopeless case and giddily happy. Everyone around these parts probably knew it, too.

Kayla left the storeroom and settled in her office to get some work done. She struggled but finally marshaled her thoughts back into order. Loving Marcelo would not deter her. He assured her of that. Her future ideas for Confetti were good and solid. She just needed to flesh some of them out. Solitude and quiet were called for and there was plenty of that to be found in her office. With a bit of luck and her laptop, she'd see the fruits of her labor by the end of the day.

Thirty minutes later, totally engrossed in her work, she didn't at first hear the knock at her door. She listened with bewilderment for the sound that had pulled her from her thoughts. A knock sounded again, a bit more forceful. She felt the screams of frustration at the back of her throat. This was the third time Alma had interrupted her. What on earth could she want now?

"Come in." She would not get up this time and open the door. She stared at the receipts in front of her.

"Hey, doll."

"Marcelo!" She rounded the desk in a flash and was in his arms. "I missed you."

Chapter 11

"You did what?" Kayla felt sure she hadn't heard correctly. They'd been engaged only a matter of days, and already her secure and happy bubble had burst. Now as she stood in Marcelo's home office she could not believe the change that had come over her fiancé.

In one fluid motion, Marcelo rose from the desk where he'd been sitting, the real-estate contract in plain sight. "I want us to travel. To see the world. Think of all the places we could visit, the history we could absorb. I can't imagine anything more…"

"You're selling the ranch." Kayla spoke with as reasonable a voice as she could manage. This could not be happening. He sounded just like her dad. Poppy had always promised that they would do and see new things when they got to the *next* place down the road. Yanking up the few roots they'd managed to put down, destroying another chance at friendship, stability and normalcy. Always looking to someplace other than where they were.

"Yes. I'm doing it for us. You don't have to give up Confetti, though. That will remain your business and will provide extra income for you as long as you wish to have it." He stated this as if his idea were obvious to Kayla. "You mentioned the other day that Alma could capably run the business without you. So, no worries there."

She watched his tall, handsome, beautifully proportioned body striding around the room, his face alight with excitement as he catalogued the pros for selling the ranch and traveling.

"But I don't want you to sell the ranch. I love it here." She walked over to the floor-to-ceiling windows and swept her arm wide to encompass the beauty outside. "Think of all your hard work, and the heritage you'll pass down to our children—a heritage from your parents for generations to come. Why would you throw all that away?"

She watched a gamut of perplexing emotions cross his face and he hesitated a moment. Hope feathered in her chest, then he shook his head and pulled her into his arms. Her mind told her to resist, but her body refused.

"We both need this, baby." He drew back and looked into her eyes. "During our first years of marriage we shouldn't be weighed down with responsibilities. Look at us. Even now, you have Confetti occupying a huge part of your day and the ranch requires long hours. Most

days I don't get to eat supper till eight or nine o'clock.
What kind of life is that for newlyweds?"

"But look how well we've made it work thus far."
Kayla could hear the desperation in her voice and wondered if he chose to ignore it, so caught up in excitement
that he clearly couldn't see that she did not want this.
"We spend quality time together and we've gotten into a
routine that fits both our schedules. We're accomplish-
ing things that people twice our age never manage."

She thought for a moment she'd gotten through to
him. He stared wordlessly at her, an expression of tenderness on his face. Then he switched all that intensity
to the contract on his desk. "No. I must do this for us—
for our family. The life we live now is no way to raise
children. They would hardly see us. We would not be
together as a family. That's how I was raised, seeing
my father only certain times during the year, and I did
not like it. Families should spend lots of time together.
I want to be there for my children at the end of the day.

"Besides, the price the buyer agreed to is over and
above what I thought the place would bring. We can
live comfortably our entire lives and we won't have the
pressure of responsibilities weighing us down. We can
buy another place someday—one that doesn't require
so much work so we can have more time together—
quality family life."

Icy fingers of dread spread through her stomach and
a dull foreboding assailed her. This scene was sicken-
ingly familiar. She took a deep breath, struggling to
maintain an even, conciliatory tone.

"So in our first disagreement, you're going to decide without my approval to do something that affects us both so drastically? Did you even ask if I wanted to quit working at Confetti?" Kayla went on the defense, hoping against hope that she could change his mind.

Gathering her into his arms he held her snugly. "Listen carefully, my love." He kissed the tip of her nose, then her eyes and finally pressed a brief but satisfying kiss on her lips. "I'm freeing myself. You can work every day if you like, but be warned. I will try and persuade you to travel with me to all the places I think we'd both enjoy." He showered gentle kisses along her jaw. "And I can be very persuasive, yes?"

Kayla felt her resolve to argue weaken as well as her knees. "Oh, yes. Very."

"Good. Then let's agree to be happy on our arranged day off from work. J.T. and Carina are barbecuing at the Citrus Queen and if I know those two, the food will be great and the fellowship fantastic." He grabbed her purse from the edge of the desk and handed it to her, turning her toward the door. "My helicopter at your service, ma'am."

Kayla remained quiet during the short trip to the family hacienda. She had not foreseen this turn of events; had not even entertained the thought of his doing something this drastic. She would have to do something to stop the sale of his beautiful place. She had no intentions of raising a family on the road. This had come clear out of the blue and as far as she was concerned it could go back where it came from.

They were greeted by Adele and driven in a golf cart the short distance to the hacienda. Kayla could tell the entire gang was here. People milled in and out of the huge wooden doors along the veranda and the noise could be heard in the next county. Accordion music mingled with Spanish guitars and someone sang badly off-key, *"aii yai yai yai, canta y no llores."* Sing and don't cry. Boy, did that ever fit the mood she was in. But she would not give up. She loved Marcelo Fuentes with the fierceness of a mama bear for her cubs. She would fight this decision with all that was in her.

"Must have been a doozie of an argument." Adele's calm voice shattered her pensive thoughts.

Kayla chuckled despite herself. "You don't argue with a Fuentes. At least this one, you don't. He has powers of persuasion that divide and conquer."

Adele harrumphed. "All three of them possess that power. At least the older two have a reliable work ethic to go with it."

Kayla followed Adele's gaze to the youngest Fuentes brother. Raoul stood with long legs wide apart and arms folded over his chest. He laughed heartily at something his brother said then turned and caught them watching him. His eyes settled on Adele and his expression stilled and grew serious. Checking Adele's response, Kayla saw her shoot him a withering glance. Raoul's eyes narrowed and his back became ramrod straight.

"What was that all about?" To her interested amazement, Adele's cheeks turned crimson.

"We don't see eye to eye very often. He gets a little touchy when I suggest that he pull his weight around here." Adele gave an impatient shrug. "Things seem to go from bad to worse if we're near each other."

"You care for him, don't you?"

"It doesn't matter if I do. I can't spend my life waiting on him to grow up and accept responsibility."

Kayla stared thoughtfully at Adele as she stalked off to the kitchen, her short curls bouncing with energy. So one Fuentes brother would not accept responsibility while the other had accepted it but now wanted to shuck it. Apparently Juan Antonio was the only normal brother. Marcelo and Raoul had major problems. Kayla chuckled in spite of herself. There had never been three brothers more self-assured, confident and successful than the three in front of her. Well, two.

She felt his breath on her cheek even as his arms closed around her waist. He whispered against her ear. "What's so funny, princess? You laughing at the locals?"

"I would never, ever laugh at—" she paused for effect "—you locals." She shrieked as he swept her off her feet and carried her to the side of the pool. "Put me down, Marcelo. I didn't bring a change of clothes." He lifted her high, but she clutched his shirtfront. "I can't swim." She allowed a note of panic to enter her voice. "You're scaring me."

He gently set her feet on the cement and held her close. "I'm sorry, *pequeñna*. I would never harm a hair on your head. I didn't know you couldn't swim."

She pulled out of his arms and hurried up the veranda steps. When she stood safely in the doorway, she turned, knowing he would be watching her. Sure enough, as she waited, barely able to refrain from laughing out loud, his dark eyes widened accusingly.

"I can..." she began and he finished.

"Swim like a fish." He started toward her and she ran, laughing triumphantly, to the nearest bathroom to hide out till someone involved him in conversation and she could make her escape.

"That's the last of the delivery. Who wants to sign?" The uniformed UPS driver thrust a clipboard at Kayla and handed her a pen.

She glanced at the paper. Twenty-one boxes. She counted each carton before adding her signature. She had thought there were twenty-two. She checked the paper again but it confirmed twenty-one, so she signed the page and handed it back to the man.

"You turned this place into a birthday store?" The man hiked up his pants and cleared his throat. "Seems awfully big for a frilly little store that sells party favors."

"We have a variety of different things, as you can see from the boxes," Kayla began, then caught his glance at the cartons stacked everywhere and realized he hadn't read the contents written on the side. "We're going to sell themes, toys. We have a catering service and chocolate-making permit."

"This was one of the best hunting stores round these parts. As the university grew, so did the town, till there was no more land to hunt on. Then the hunters went elsewhere. It's a shame it closed." He checked her signature, then ambled to the door. "Best o' luck on the new business."

"Thanks. Come back and visit us."

"Will do."

Kayla didn't think she could become more discouraged, but the man had actually managed to increase her annoyance. Then she felt guilty for blaming her bad mood on an innocent man. She needed someone to talk to but Alma was out of town on a buying spree and her other employees were too young to understand.

Just then the door opened. "Hey, chica? Wanna go get some lunch?"

"Carina, you just made my day." She took her purse from the bottom desk drawer and locked it back. "I am pity-partying it so bad today I'm making myself sick."

"Well, you can tell me all about it over soup and salad."

When they were seated and the waitress took their drink order, Carina propped her arms on the table. 'So why the sad face?"

"Marcelo wants to sell the ranch. Can you believe that?"

"Tonio told me last night. He and Raoul hashed it out and finally decided to back Marcelo. I don't think they're happy about it, but it is his place and he has a right to do whatever he wants with it."

"Even if it destroys us?" Kayla's voice caught and she had to take a drink of tea.

Carina reached and patted her hand. Ever the consoler. The peacemaker. She was such a good friend. "Why would selling the ranch destroy you?"

She shared her childhood story with Carina and sure enough Carina comforted her and offered her advice.

"Talk to him. Tell him how you feel. Don't let what happened to Tonio and me happen to you."

"But we don't have the same problem as you. We *are* talking it out—only he's not listening. It's like he's suddenly a driven man."

"How do you mean?"

"He brings home brochures for overseas-travel packages." Kayla could feel the tears clogging her throat. "I'm getting so scared."

"So traveling is something you don't want to consider?"

"I get physically sick at the very thought. Vacations I can handle. Moving from place to place with nowhere to call home would torture me."

"I wonder why he is entertaining this idea of selling."

"His mother heard us in a bit of an argument the other night and she asked him why. He said there should be nothing he couldn't give up for me. That was his description of true love. But I don't want that. I love the ranch. It feels like home. I'm not asking him to give it up."

"And you've explained this clearly?"

"Yes. He says that I should be thankful. That he is doing this totally for me and our future children, and he doesn't understand why I can't be happy for us." Kayla moved the food around on her plate, her appetite gone.

"I don't understand. That doesn't make sense." Carina seemed as confused as Kayla.

"I made the mistake of saying Alma could run Confetti without me and he even uses that to make his point." Kayla felt like screaming in frustration. "I wrestle with this every waking hour. I vowed never to live like my childhood and I can tell you now, if just the thought of traveling makes me crazy, think what an actual lifestyle of it would do."

"I can imagine."

"Carina, what am I going to do? I love him more than life itself."

"I don't know, sweetie, but I will be praying that God changes his mind and that you will get some answers."

"I guess I'll have to choose." She gulped hard, hot tears slipping down her cheeks.

"Oh, Kayla. Let's get out of here."

In the car, Carina sat sideways in the seat and took Kayla's hands. "We're going to pray, so close your eyes."

Had Kayla not been so heartbroken she would have laughed. She obeyed.

"Lord, I'm still not much good at praying diplomatically, so please hear my prayer because it is from the heart. My sweet friend is troubled over the relationship with the man she's engaged to be married to. Father, we love him so much. He's kind and considerate and maybe just a bit misguided. Will You check out what's going on in his head and change his mind? And we ask, Heavenly Father, that You gather sweet Kayla in Your arms and give her peace in her heart. Give her instructions on how to proceed and help her to do Your will only. In Jesus's name, Amen."

Back at Confetti, Kayla considered the words of Carina's prayer. She needed to find God's will for her life. She surely had been more faithful to church and she and Marcelo had discussed openly their thoughts on serving God with the family they hoped the Lord would bless them with. His mother, Marta, had shared mistakes she and his dad had made and advised them not to go in certain directions. To learn from her mistakes.

One night she and Marta sat arm in arm on the sofa as Marcelo expounded on the good life they would have, his eyes were glowing and his voice excited. That's the night Kayla knew she couldn't stand in the way of his dreams. This was something he wanted to do and he had that right. His mother tried to explain it when they were alone at Confetti the next day. She reminded Kayla that Marcelo had worked since he was eighteen years old; that maybe he was tired of the stress and responsibility.

Now all Kayla had to do was figure out where she stood in all this. Could she bear to live her childhood again? Even more, could she inflict all the hurt and confusion that that lifestyle would bring on her children? If there was only someone who could give her the answers. She felt God was telling her He had the answers. All she needed to do was go to Him. "I know You have the answers, Lord. I'm just afraid of what they are."

Chapter 12

Marcelo stared at the woman standing in front of him, her head bowed, fingers shredding the tissue she held. Torn by conflicting emotions she couldn't or wouldn't share with him. At the moment he wasn't sure which choice motivated her. But a permanent sorrow seemed to weigh them both down.

"What are you saying, Kayla? That you don't love me anymore?" He tried to soften the strained tone of his voice. A heaviness centered in his chest. He rubbed the area distractedly. She raised her eyes, large glittering ovals of repudiation.

"You know better than that." She spoke in a broken whisper.

Marcelo nearly choked on a desperate laugh. "How, Kayla?" He flung his hands out in despair. "You're leaving me. How exactly does that make me know you love me?" He watched the first tear roll down her cheek. In one forward motion he clasped her tightly to him. She melted against him, her arms locking around his waist. A powerful sigh lifted his chest and settled in the region of his heart. This felt right. He should have taken her in his arms sooner. The mere touch of someone you love could comfort in ways words could not. He would remember that.

He felt her lingering kiss against his neck; she seemed to breathe him in, then her gaze swept over his face as if memorizing it. Without looking away, she backed out of his grasp. The door closed softly behind her, leaving him gutted, the shock rendering him immobile.

Kayla drove across the long bay bridge to South Padre Island and for the first time in over two hours, took notice of the scenery around her. A barge pulling a tugboat passed under the bridge below. To the south she saw a charter fishing boat returning to port. She passed the Padre Island sign and turned left, following the instructions of the voice on the GPS.

There was a hollowness inside her; a mindless confusion with no direction whatsoever. A sob escaped and she felt tears gather but none fell. She wouldn't fall apart till she was alone, off the highway and where no one would see the depths of despair in her soul. The computerized woman's voice instructed her to take the next right; she had reached her destination. Moments later she signed for a nonsmoking, no-pet room and received her key.

She took the elevator to the sixth floor of the hotel and somehow found the door with her room number and inserted the card key. It beeped and did not open. She tried again, making sure the arrows were facing her and downward. Still nothing. She laid her head against the door. She wanted to beat the door, to scream at the little light beside the card slot that refused to turn green. Taking a deep calming breath she tried again and mercifully the light flashed green and she entered her room. She didn't even check the layout; just fell on the bed, deep racking sobs shuddering through her body. Bereft, absolutely alone, with a hole the size of Texas in her heart.

She could still smell him, feel the stubble on his cheek against her face. A part of her had been ripped away; her mind was languid, without hope. Everything in life she'd ever loved had been taken from her, except Confetti. First her beloved parents, now her handsome, ever-smiling Marcelo. She closed her eyes, reliving the pain of that final scene. His dark eyes that most often shone with some form of mischief or tomfoolery, a teasing glint as he cajoled her into a better mood, had dimmed, first with anger then confusion, and as she'd closed the door, huge pools of pain. His jaw had clenched tight yet a tremor moved over his lips and that almost shattered her resolve.

With a moan of distress she hugged a pillow to her chest. Her life had been a bitter battle. Not much pleasure had been afforded her and she wondered briefly if God even cared. Like an old wound that ached on a rainy day, she remembered the years of loneliness that had been her constant companion. And now it sank cold tentacles into her anguished soul. She pulled the bed-spread over her and yielded to the misery of an aching heart. She wasn't up to coping and it was pointless to deny the sense of permanent sorrow weighing her down.

For the next two weeks she nursed her broken heart, at times her thoughts jagged and painful, at other times with a steadfast and serene peace. She walked along the beach in the early morning hours before the sun rose over the horizon. The sound of the ocean waves, the seagull cries and salt air calmed her troubled mind. In the evenings she climbed out on the rock jetty and sat until sunset and she examined the unfulfilled dreams and plans for her life. It wasn't lost on her that she had chosen not to live her life in a way that made her extremely unhappy. And she was not unaware that she'd lost nearly everything that meant anything to her. And while no rhyme or reason emerged from the chaos of her decision, one good thing had taken place. She now walked in renewed faith—stronger, secure in the fact that God would guide her as long as she sought His help.

She'd read the Psalms and one verse especially had encouraged her greatly. In chapter 25, verse 12 it said *What man is he that feareth the Lord; him shall he teach in the way that he shall choose*. She had a healthy respect for God and she trusted implicitly that God would help her make good choices. And right now, God was the only certainty in her life.

Her bags packed and checkout complete, she loaded everything into her car trunk and slammed it shut. She hated to leave but Confetti pulled at her, cajoling her to come home. She could hardly wait to get among the party bags, the colorful balloons, the bags of confetti and favors. She'd written down several ideas for expanding into full-time catering and party planning. The store connected to Confetti had gone out of business and she hoped to rent it and make a play area for birthday parties or *Quinceañeras*. She'd need to hire more workers. That would not be a problem since sales had tripled the last quarter.

She slowed to a mere thirty-five as she passed through the small towns of Port Isabel and Los Fresnos. The one thought heavy on her mind was where she would live. If the Lord permitted, this would be the last place she ever moved. With His help, she would never be homeless again. Clicking the hands-free phone connection on her steering wheel she called Juan Antonio and asked him to meet her at the Citrus Queen. She then checked in with Alma and told her she needed a few more days off from work to find a place to live and finish wedding arrangements with Carina.

She took the long, palm-lined drive to the hacienda. The road needed to be patched and paved over again but she thought it added to the old-South flavor of the place. Foliage hung from the tops of the palms, begging to be trimmed, and even though they were entering the winter season, the temps hadn't dropped enough to kill the grass and it needed to be mowed. She wondered briefly if this was what Adele meant when she said Raoul needed to pull his weight. She parked beside the steps that led up to the veranda. Juan Antonio's truck sat on the other side. She dreaded this meeting.

Carina met her at the door, compassion lining her

beautiful face. She hooked her arm through Kayla's and guided her past a confused-looking Juan Antonio into the room they'd set up to do the sewing and bouquet making for Carina's wedding. Adele stood just inside the door with yards of satin wrapped around both arms and her smile lit a tiny flicker of hope in Kayla's bruised heart. Just maybe she wouldn't lose the friendship with these two.

"So what happened?" Carina lost no time in frivolities. She cut straight to the chase.

"Yeah, we looked around and you were gone. No word of your whereabouts or nothing. We've been worried." Adele dumped the cloth on the table beside her and clasped Kayla in a brief, hard hug. "Don't ever do that again."

Kayla felt tears gather in her eyes. "I'm sorry. I wasn't thinking straight." She waved a hand in the air. "I wasn't thinking at all." Her voice dropped to a mere whisper. "All I could do was feel."

Carina swept aside the fabric Adele had dropped on the table and pulled the chair out for Kayla to sit. She chose the chair beside her and Adele the one across. "Tonio said you broke the engagement. Why?"

Adele added, "He put the ranch up for sale. Was that because you broke off the engagement?" She pulled on a tight curl and released it, a sure sign she was upset.

"No, that's *why* I broke it off." Kayla sought for words to explain. It was harder than she thought. "My entire childhood I never lived more than six months in one place. I need roots. And I won't raise a family on the road. Marcelo would not listen. He's dead set on traveling the world, and while I realize some men do this before they settle down and raise a family, it's not something I want to do."

"Surely some form of compromise can be reached. You two love each other. You can't throw that away." Carina stroked the top of Kayla's hand lying on the table, soothing and calming like the sweet lady she was.

"I explained, but it was like he wanted to believe me yet resolved to do just the opposite. I've never seen him act like that. We discussed it several times and I'd get the feeling he agreed totally with me then he'd take me in his arms and promise to never let anything stand between us." Kayla heard the exasperation in her voice but wanted her friends to understand.

"It's that girl." Adele smacked a hand on the table and Kayla jumped. Whether from the noise or the statement she couldn't be sure.

"What girl?" Carina asked.

"What did you say?" Kayla asked at the same time.

"Her name was Larisa and they were engaged. She was all wrong for Marc, but he asked her to marry him anyway. She handed him a list of things he had to change before they married and one of them was travel."

"But why would that be a problem?" Carina evidently hadn't heard the story because she asked all the questions. Kayla hadn't known of the engagement and sat stunned, absorbing the fact that Marcelo had loved another woman.

Had Kayla not been crushed by the news, she would have giggled out loud. Carina sounded like she wanted to fix the problem with this Larisa girl and Marcelo.

She would make a great mother with the natural talent for nurturing and fixing things.

"But she gave him an ultimatum." Adele's disgust warned them of horrible things to come, at least in her estimation.

Kayla heard Carina's quick intake of breath and knew they were of the same mindset. You didn't issue ultimatums to the Fuentes men, although they felt free to issue them. Juan Antonio had issued an ultimatum to Carina and it nearly destroyed their relationship.

Kayla clasped her hands together to keep them from shaking. Her beloved Marcelo with the laughing eyes that touched her very soul had loved another woman so much he'd asked her to marry him. The woman had issued an ultimatum, he'd refused and they were no longer together. She cleared her throat but her voice still sounded strangled.

"What was it?"

"Her or the ranch." Adele nearly spat the words, accentuating the annoyance she felt.

Kayla merely stared at Adele tongue-tied. Carina on the other hand had no problem voicing her opinion. "How selfish. Then he is better off without her. Could she not see how much of his life he'd already put into building a home and security for them?"

"Apparently not. But that was several years ago and he hadn't built the house yet, but there was a cabin he remodeled and it was quite beautiful. I think Flipper lives there now. Anyway, she kept the ring. She had dollar signs in her eyes and thought Marc would finance her jet-setting lifestyle. I was glad to see the backside of her as she left. Silly woman."

The irony of the situation was not lost on Kayla. One woman he loved wanted him to get rid of the ranch; the other woman he loved wanted him to keep it.

A brief knock, then the door opened to admit Juan Antonio. "Sorry to interrupt, but, Kayla, you wanted to see me?"

"Yes," she said faintly and stood and walked toward him. Her body and mind were finally moving together. When they were on the other side of the closed door she removed an envelope from her purse and handed it to him. "Will you see that Marcelo gets this?" At his nod she continued. "He needs to file it as soon as possible."

"I'll take it to him now. I'm headed over that way." He paused as if uncertain how to continue. "Kayla, I'm sorry for whatever caused the rift between you two. Since he met you he's been the happiest I've ever known Marcelo to be. I hope you get things straightened out. Don't waste precious time. If you can fix things then do it. Life is too short to be separated from those we love."

Too choked up to speak, Kayla could only nod. She all but ran to her car. She needed a moment to absorb all the information she'd just heard. It took her all of two seconds to realize she had nowhere to go. Again! Her annoyance increased when she found that her hands were shaking. Screams of frustration lodged at the back of her throat. She latched on to the steering wheel, pressed back against the headrest and gave rein to them, yelling out her frustrations. She beat the steering wheel and rocked back and forth on the seat. How could she be homeless again? She had vowed never to let this happen. She was furious—first with herself, then with Marcelo. Why could he not have loved her enough to know that she needed security, stability?

Carina appeared at the top of the steps so Kayla lifted her phone to signal she needed to make a call. Carina nodded and returned to the house. Kayla wasn't up to talking to anyone just yet.

So Marcelo had been engaged to a woman who demanded that he sell his ranch. Kayla on the other hand, had pretty much demanded that he keep it. Now if she could figure out why he wouldn't give it up for the first fiancée but would for the second she just might understand what was going on in his mind.

Dare she hope? She had broken things off with a finality that most likely shut all doors from any future openings anytime soon. She struggled a moment with her conscience. Had she acted rashly? She closed her eyes and remembered the pain in his expression the day she walked out. "Stop agonizing over it, Kayla. You've moved on," she spoke aloud. *Not so,* her heart whispered back. "And what about all the time at the beach? You made lists and plans and resolved to put all this behind you and make sure it never happened again. What about all the pep talks and soul searching? The catalog of things that would not have worked anyway."

Wearied by confusion and the disquiet in her heart, she sought for solid ground. A port in the storm. She was not disappointed. The quieter she became, the more the more the scripture spoke to her: *Come unto Me, all ye that labour and are heavy laden, and I will give you rest.* Her mind went back to a verse in Psalm 25 that she'd read over and over at Padre Island. *The troubles of my heart are enlarged; Oh bring thou me out of my distresses.*

A sense of strength slowly began to fill her and the overwhelming despair lessened. With abrupt clarity she somehow knew things would be okay; God was on His throne and she was His child. She lingered a few moments more, basking in the peace that enveloped her like a hug. A cry of praise sprang from her lips.

She ran up the steps and entered the hacienda with a lighter heart. Carina and Adele paused midstride and stared at her. "Can we talk?"

They took the exact same seats as before and Kayla began slowly, feeling her way along, voicing her doubt that she'd done the right thing in breaking the engagement.

As usual, Carina took the initiative, asking the difficult questions, cutting to the chase.

"Are you saying you had ulterior motives when you broke the engagement?"

"No. I had no motives at all, but I did hope he would come after me." Kayla tried to disguise her insecurities in front of her friends but finally gave up, needing to come clean so she could get help. "Was I wrong to think we had something so special he wouldn't let me go?"

Carina hesitated then said slowly, weighing her words carefully, "No, that wasn't wrong, but it was deceitful if you did it to make him do your will."

"Did you plan the whole thing?" Adele's voice held a vague sense of disapproval.

"I didn't plan at all. I acted instinctively."

"Then what are you trying to say? That you want us to decide whether you handled things badly?"

"Yes. I guess so." At Adele's look of disbelief she defended her actions. "This was not premeditated. He wouldn't change his mind about selling the ranch and I refused to raise a family without a home."

"So neither of you would compromise for the good of your life together." Carina's way of clarifying things always surprised Kayla.

"Something like that."

"Well I'm not an expert on love—" Adele's voice was heavy with sarcasm "—but it seems to me if it's true love it's worth fighting for and if the one I loved ran away when the going got tough, I'd never have trust in that person again."

Kayla's breath caught in her throat and she laid her head on both arms folded on the table. Carina patted her arm and pushed a tissue into her hand. "Don't cry. We have to get to the bottom of this or you'll never be confident of your decision. It will eat at you and cause you misery and pain. Believe me, I know. Been there, done that."

Kayla wiped her eyes and Adele reached for her hand. "I'm sorry, Kayla. I'm the last person to judge your motives or decisions. I can't even catch a man, much less keep him."

"Please don't apologize. I value your opinion and I needed to hear what you said."

"How do you feel about Marcelo now?"

"Oh, Carina. I still love him with all my heart, soul

and body. I love so much about him. His care of Marta and the way he looks out for Juan Antonio and Raoul."

"So what did you hope to accomplish by leaving?"

"There was no hoping. I felt my only option was to leave. Somewhere, deep down, though, I hoped he'd come after me and tell me he'd take the hacienda off the market and the engagement would be back on. But he didn't."

"None of us knew where you had gone. I called your phone a couple dozen times but no answer." Adele's frustrations were evident by the way her voice rose. "You broke all our hearts. We love you, Kayla, and you're part of our family now. Families stick together."

"Adele, if Marcelo doesn't want me anymore, we can't be family."

"So if he does want you, will you go back to him on his terms?" Carina's gentle questioning caused tears to swell up and start a slow trek down Kayla's cheeks.

"I'm not sure I can go back to that lifestyle. It would destroy me and I'd become bitter, eventually making Marcelo's life miserable. But…" She paused, holding raw emotions in check. "I'm not sure I'll survive without him." Sobs shook her body and both girls wrapped their arms around her.

She controlled the crying jag and Carina took charge. "Let's get our minds on something else. We can either work on bouquets here or run to Confetti and make some chocolate. What's it to be?"

"Chocolate," both Adele and Kayla answered in unison.

When they walked into Confetti sometime later,

Alma looked up and exclaimed, "Well, praise the Lord." She grabbed Kayla and wrapped her in a tight hug. "How are you, sweet girl?"

"I'm feeling pretty low, but I'll survive. I always do."

Alma turned the sign on the door to Closed and they made their way back to the kitchen. Quite a few changes had been made since they'd first opened and now commercial stoves and ovens gleamed silver, clean and bright. She prepared the three different chocolate mixes they'd chosen for signature pieces for Carina's bridal shower. Alma turned the contraption on that held the burner and the dispenser and the others crowded close, catching any little bit that overflowed from the allotted slots.

They began to giggle and lick their fingers, Adele making her own designs as the extra chocolate was discarded. "Remember *I Love Lucy* where she worked on the assembly line and she wasn't fast enough and she crammed chocolates down her shirt and in her hat?"

Kayla felt the first hysterical giggle bubble up in her throat. "Then she crammed her hat back on when the boss lady came through the door."

Carina held her side she laughed so hard. She crammed chocolates in her mouth, mimicking Lucy and Ethel.

"Wasn't that when the boss lady told the man to make the assembly line go faster?" Carina nodded her head in answer to Alma's question, choked on the chocolates and blew them out of her mouth. They landed on Adele's shirtfront and Carina's look of horror set them all off in peals of laughter.

Kayla started twisting frantically, needing badly to use the bathroom. Giggling always did that to her. She plopped down on the floor, her legs crossed. For some reason that garnered more laughter and when they finally got control, they all sat on the floor with Kayla.

Kayla was the first to speak. "That felt good."

"Yes, it did. I'm sorry about your blouse, Adele." Carina waved a hand in the air. "The wedding arrangements have driven me crazy and even though I've enjoyed them, I will be so glad when December arrives and I can marry the man of my dreams and stop all this madness." She reached above her head for the container of chocolates. She took one, then passed them around the circle. "Kayla, these are possibly the best chocolates I've ever tasted. Why don't you market them all over the world? You'd make a killing."

"But that's why I can't. If I marketed them in bulk, I'd have to add preservatives. Since these will be used as we make them, there are no preservatives, which accounts for the rich chocolaty taste."

"Amazing, isn't it—" Alma stated calmly "—what chocolate and a good laugh will do?"

"Yeah, I've about decided to move on. I'm tired of waiting on Raoul to grow up and act like a man. We're going backward instead of forward and I don't want to waste any more time. He's never going to love me and I'm tired of feeling like a loser," Adele said. The girls could tell her pride had been seriously bruised by Raoul's behavior.

"Why are men so blind?" Kayla felt the sting of Marcelo's insensitivity all over again.

"They have a good woman in front of them and they mess it up."

All three women turned to stare at Alma. She turned a vivid scarlet.

Kayla crawled across the floor to her side. She put a comforting arm around her friend's shoulder. "What happened, Alma?"

"Yeah, you can tell us. It will go no further. And we know people, so if we need to break his knees just say the word." Adele's tough stance caused Kayla's giggles to start again but she quickly squashed them.

"Please tell us, Alma, we only want to help." No one could say no to the lovely Carina so Kayla settled more closely to her friend in case she needed a shoulder to cry on. This was going to be good. Friends helping friends. She loved having friends.

When no sound came forth they all three stared at Alma. She looked each one of them in the eye. They sat in an uncomfortable silence, waiting, giving Alma time to gather her thoughts. She must really be having a difficult time. They all kept darting glances at her and finally she huffed, "What in pig Latin are ya'll talking about?"

Kayla shook her head. "But you just said, you know, about the man having a good woman in front of him. All that stuff."

Alma's lips puckered with annoyance. "I was talking about your two fellas." She pointed at Kayla and Adele. "When and if I ever fall in love, I'll make sure he's not related to the Fuentes brothers in any manner. Those men put their women through the ringer." At

Carina's attempted protest, Alma raised a finger in the air and shushed her. "Don't even deny it or take up for J.T., Carina. He broke your heart with that marriage ultimatum and you know it. Now Marc has gone and crushed Kayla's spirit, and Raoul…" She paused and gathered more steam. "Someone needs to take him to the woodshed and kick his sorry behind."

They sat quiet, stunned by Alma's words. No one ever spoke badly about the Fuentes men. After all, they were some of the best in the Rio Grande Valley. Finally Adele raised her hand and Alma gave her a smacking high five. Carina tried to suppress a giggle. Kayla curled up on the floor laughing and Alma and Adele jumped to their feet and did a jig.

Later that night, Kayla pulled on pajamas and crawled into the bed. Adele refused to let her stay in a hotel, insisting there were too many unoccupied bedrooms and baths at the Citrus Queen. Her load had been lightened a bit tonight. She said a brief prayer of thanks.

Chapter 13

Marcelo again stared at the plain manila envelope
Kayla had sent via Juan Antonio. He'd refused to open
it. J.T. had said it needed to be filed so it was probably some kind of legal paper releasing the items they'd
bought together. Or it could be a demand for her share.
He neither wanted to know which it was nor did he care.

It had been two weeks, three days, six hours and
forty-seven minutes since he'd seen her last. Not that
he was counting or anything; it had just been that long
since he'd felt human. His normal happy spirits had disappeared when she walked out the door. He hadn't asked
anyone where she'd gone but apparently they hadn't
known because sooner or later all of them asked him
if he knew. That had given him a moment of unease,
but he'd tamped it down, daring it to raise its caring-
for-everyone-else head again. He tossed the offending

envelope in the bottom drawer of the desk and turned the key. Some things were best locked away against the light of day.

He walked to the kitchen which still bore evidence of Kayla's residence here. Her juicer sat on the countertop beside his Keurig one-cup coffee machine. Yogurt lined his refrigerator shelves. When he crossed through to the living room her lap blanket lay neatly on the upholstered rocking chair. If he picked it up he would smell her perfume. He knew this because he had wrapped himself in it when the misery became too great to endure.

The hurt had been replaced with anger. Anger that became a scalding fury. He longed to hurt her like she'd hurt him. A circle of ice seemed to have surrounded his heart. After the first week, he deliberately shut out any awareness of her. But for the first few days, he had to drag himself from bed, barely eating and being so rude to his mother she'd left and gone to Raoul's. Now, he made it through each day the best he could. At least he knew Kayla was safe. He'd cruised by Confetti several times a day the first week but her car was never there. He worried over where she could be. It wasn't like her to leave her store but he hadn't once thought she'd leave him. So much for his ability to judge character.

When Kayla walked out he turned to the next greatest love of his life. His ranch. He buried himself in work. He didn't know why he was working so hard on a place he was going to sell; he just knew he had to keep moving. Hard work left him too exhausted at night to lie awake and think. Flipper's wife had taken to preparing meals again when his mother left. He gained back a little strength from the good meals and life went on.

Thanksgiving came and went and he stayed home from the usual meal and festivities at the Citrus Queen. He wasn't good company for anyone. Besides, Kayla would probably be invited and he had no desire to see her. Or so he told himself. It couldn't be because he feared the raw sores of an aching heart might split open again.

"Boss, do you have the accounts-payable ledger for the grain and molasses?"

He hadn't even heard Flip enter the house. It had been like this too long. He would get his act together today. His foreman had carried the load, taking up the slack, but it was time he started calling the shots again.

"Sure." He unlocked the bottom drawer and removed the manila envelope and the ledger that lay under it. Flip left the room and Marcelo sank down into the chair, weary and worn. He hadn't read his Bible in several days and his faith level had a virus.

Kayla and Adele carried on a mildly boring conversation relaxing in the deck chairs around the pool. Carina sat at the table, laptop open and surfing the boards on interesting things. They'd all worked today and for varying reasons all of them were tired and dragging. Kayla just couldn't get her energy level back up and she'd lost weight. Carina had ten days left till her Christmas wedding and anything bad that could happen had happened.

Raoul had not been home for several nights and

though he and Adele had never been sweethearts, anyone with any sense at all knew they were a romance
fixing to happen. Adele worried over him but right now
she was fighting mad because they were in such need
of his expertise in the orchards.

They heard Juan Antonio's truck pull into the driveway. When he walked in he announced, "You're not
going to believe what's happened." Whatever it was
evidently made him very happy. He leaned down for
a quick kiss from Carina. "Marcelo took the ranch off
the market."

Kayla sprang from the lounge chair. "He did?" She
took a quick breath of utter astonishment. "Why?"

"He said he did it for himself."

"I have to go see him. This means we can be together." Kayla's fatigue vanished like the dew.

She ran around the pool deck ignoring Carina's
warning voice as she called, "Kayla, wait."

She had waited long enough. She drove like a ma-
niac from the aged hacienda with its faded glamour to
the new one that she loved so dearly. She took the road
to the line shack then drove past it on to Marcelo's. She
ran from the car and slowed only to close the front door
behind her. She found him at the desk poring over fi-
nancial ledgers.

"Marcelo?" Her breath caught in her throat as she
felt her heart pounding.

He jumped up, the chair crashing behind him. "From
now on I'm going to lock that door if it's the last thing
I do. I'm sick and tired of unwanted company crashing my workday."

"I'm sorry. I didn't realize you didn't want company." Hungrily her eyes took in the ruggedness of his features and the unkempt hair. His beard had grown out, and lay smooth along the jawline and chin. He'd lost a little weight, too, and though he looked a bit wild she thought him the most handsome man she'd ever seen.

"Why on earth would you think I wanted you here, Kayla?" She flinched at his rudeness but stood quietly while he righted his chair. Her knees trembled but even with him angry she knew there was no other place she wanted to be.

"I'm sorry, Marcelo. I made a bad decision, but so did you. Now that you're not selling the house we can be together. Doesn't that make you happy?"

He stared at her like she had two heads. "Are you insane?" His voice rose an octave. "You think I want to marry someone who runs at the first sign of trouble? Not on your life. You left me, Kayla, like our life together mattered not one iota. I loved you. Do you have any inkling what that means? You tore my heart out and stomped it on the ground. You can forget about there ever being a 'you and me'"— he made quote signs with his hands "—ever again. It won't happen."

She heard the hurt in his strong voice and the extent of her mistake began to sink in. "But, Marcelo, the very reason we were torn apart was because you put the ranch up for sale. Juan Antonio said you took it off the market. I would never have left had you not insisted on selling the ranch."

"Why didn't you stop me, Kayla, instead of running like your parents did all your life? You're the same as them. Too irresponsible to stand and face problems head-on." He turned his back on her and faced the window. His words cut to the quick.

"That's not fair and you know it. I tried to stop you. From the first time you mentioned it I repeatedly told you I didn't want you to sell the ranch. But did you listen?" Kayla had her own ax to grind and she allowed the hurt and bitterness to enter her voice. "No, you continued to fill our home with travel brochures. You talked non-stop about all the places you wanted to visit. How could I stop you if that's what you longed to do? I loved you. I wanted you to be happy. I couldn't deny you that."

"But I didn't want to sell the ranch. I was doing it for you."

"Where on earth did you get the idea that I wanted to travel? That's what's bugged me about this entire thing. You know my background and that my parents moved all the time. Why would you think I'd prefer that kind of lifestyle?" She waited with bated breath to see if he'd mention the Larisa girl he'd been engaged to. It still hurt that he'd never told her about his previous engagement.

"I needed to put you first. I didn't want the ranch to ever come between us. Is that so difficult to understand?" His voice had lost some of its anger.

"Yes, actually, it is since I never once suggested the ranch was coming between us. When did you stop seeing me, Marcelo, and start letting Larisa guide your decisions?"

He let out a long, audible breath. "Someone's misinformed you badly. Larisa never even made it in the running. While we briefly contemplated becoming engaged, it was one temper tantrum after the other. She ranted and raved, and demanded that I sell the ranch, but never once was I tempted to give up my inheritance. She was like a mosquito. Aggravating. And her bite was poison. My heart was not involved, even though I thought it was at the time."

Kayla's confidence spiraled upward. If he hadn't loved Larisa, then she was his first love. Wasn't that a sign? Didn't people say you never got over your first love?

"When did your heart stop being involved with me, Marcelo?"

"I guess about the same time you walked out on me without a backward look."

Bravely she walked to where he stood, looking out the window. She rubbed his arm in a gentle caress. He jumped like he'd been shot.

"Get out of here, Kayla. You threw my love back in my face and that's something I can't forgive. I'm sorry. We're through."

Kayla's mind was congested with doubts and fears. They'd never had many disagreements and in this one, she couldn't figure out which of them was most wrong. Seemed to her he was the pot calling the kettle black.

"You know what, Marcelo? Yes, I was the one to walk away from the life you offered, but you were the one who walked away from me. You let Larisa's choices determine our future, instead of asking me what I wanted. You're a fraud." She turned and walked a second time out the door. It took her forever to get to her car. The longest walk in history. It was a good thing her

car had a push-button starter. She'd never have managed
to insert a key; her hands shook too badly.

Marcelo sank into the desk chair. He ran a hand over
his beard. He felt poleaxed. Spasms of alarm shook his
body. Was he as guilty as Kayla accused of destroying
their relationship? Had he misjudged her so harshly?

How had she learned about Larisa? Since falling in
love with Kayla he realized that what he'd had with
Larisa was an infatuation, a crush, nothing like the
heartrending feelings he had for Kayla. Even breathing was difficult without Kayla.

Slowly, bit by painful bit, the truth began to sink in.
He *had* allowed what happened with Larisa to color
his thoughts and decisions about Kayla. "Why?" he
groaned. He knew why but he needed to tell Kayla.

The simple truth was that he hadn't loved Larisa and
she would never have been more important than his
ranch. It was for that very reason that he'd felt the need
to prove to Kayla that nothing or no one would ever be
more important to him than her. He'd driven her away
because he'd been afraid she'd leave him, too.

*There is no fear in love; but perfect love casteth
out fear: because fear hath torment. He that feareth
is not made perfect in love.* He'd learned that verse in
Vacation Bible School when he'd turned nine and was
struggling with the absence of his father. It had been
a promise then that kept him safe and secure at night
allowing him to sleep. It was judgment now, pointing
out his wrong actions, convicting him of his weakness.
And was he ever tormented.

He tore the manila envelope open, curious as to what items Kayla would have taken and the ones she'd have kept. Surprise siphoned the blood from his face. He read the pages in front of him carefully. She'd signed the deed of her property over to him. The land he'd tried to buy because of the natural water rights. He ran a hand through his hair. *The land she'd vowed never to part with because it gave her roots.* How could he have been so stupid? He rubbed his thumb over the State of Texas seal. The deed had been notarized.

He felt a deep sense of shame. He had vowed in his heart to take care of Kayla, to right the wrongs of her past. And here he had tried to force a lifestyle on her that she'd hated. He needed to find her, to make things right.

Just as he started toward the door, J.T. walked in. "You're as white as a sheet, man." Juan Antonio's voice shattered Marcelo's last nerve.

Marcelo strode toward Juan Antonio, his arm pointing to the exit. "Turn yourself right back around and get out of here. If one more person enters this house uninvited I'm going to sucker punch them." He grabbed Juan Antonio by the arm, propelling him through the office toward the front door. Juan Antonio did a quick right turn and walked out of Marcelo's grasp. When Marcelo lunged after him, Juan Antonio picked up a pool cue that was propped against the fireplace. He held it in a defense position.

"Calm down, Markie-poo. Did someone lick the red off your sucker?" Juan Antonio taunted, a huge grin splitting his face.

Marcelo swung but Juan Antonio trapped his arm across the pool stick, wrapping it behind Marcelo's back. "Stop being an idiot or I'll mess up your pretty-girl face. Your choice. Personally it doesn't matter to me, but Carina will be mad if you have both eyes blacked shut in our wedding pictures." When Marcelo didn't even struggle he shoved him away, hanging on to the pool stick just in case.

Marcelo buried his hands in his hair and collapsed into a chair. He propped his elbows on his legs, his clasped hands falling between them. Dejected, his misery so acute it was a physical pain. "I've lost her, J.T. She was just here and I made her leave."

"Oh, man. I'm sorry. So that's why you're being a jerk. What'd you do this time?"

He filled Juan Antonio in on all the ugly details; embellishing his part in the demise of his engagement to the only girl he would ever love.

"Then fix it, Marc. That doesn't sound too bad. Carina and I were separated for months, long, agonizing, gut-wrenching months. Don't let that happen to you and Kayla. Crawl, beg, prostate yourself, whatever it takes, but get her back."

"She signed the deed of her land over to me, notarized and all. It's final."

"Sounds serious."

"It's a gesture of surrender, right?"

"You're asking me? I'm a bigger dummy than you when it comes to understanding women's minds. I'm barely learning what keeps Carina happy and you want me to tell you what yours thinks? Ha. That's a case of the blind leading the blind."

Marcelo felt as if his head might explode. "Are you gonna help me or not? Surely you know something about romance. You're getting married two Saturdays from now, for crying out loud. Help me, I'm in a mess." With a bounce he was out of the chair, pacing in front of the long windows. "My head is splitting. My vision's blurred. I feel like my heart might be dying and I could cry like a baby. Have mercy, man. Give me something."

"Go find her. I overheard her telling the girls that she hoped you would come after her. That her heart broke when you didn't." Juan Antonio thought for a moment then continued, "She said she felt certain you'd never let her go, but apparently she was wrong. You didn't even put up a fight. Her words, not mine."

"And?"

Marcelo wanted to beat J.T. to a pulp. He took too long thinking. "She said you were the first man she'd ever kissed, that you taught her what love really meant. Oh, and that she thought you should pay for my honeymoon since you messed up royally with her."

Weary, slow but cherishing the news that he'd been her first kiss, it took Marcelo a few seconds to absorb the last part of Juan Antonio's statement.

He laughed at the wide-eyed innocent look in his younger brother's eyes.

"Ah, now that's more like the brother I grew up with." The huskiness in Juan Antonio's voice touched Marcelo's heart. They'd been there for each other through thick and thin.

He left the house and headed for his truck. He was going to bring his woman home. But just so it was clearly understood who was still boss in the family, he allowed J.T. to catch up with him then planted a sucker punch to the stomach.

Juan Antonio doubled over clutching his abdomen. "Aww, man, why'd you go do a fool thing like that?"

"That's for not telling me that Kayla was at the Citrus Queen."

"But a stomach punch will hurt me all through my honeymoon."

"Crybaby."

Juan Antonio finally made it to an upright position. His eyes sparkled with the promise of revenge. He hobbled to his truck and as he swung up into the seat he threatened, "I'm telling Kayla you hit me."

Marcelo laughed heartily. That had always been their last defense. He watched J.T. back up and spin his tires as he floorboarded it down the drive. Then it hit him. He hadn't said he was telling Mother Marcelo hit him, he was telling Kayla. He jumped into his Ford, intent on getting to Kayla before his younger brother. He passed him about two miles before the Citrus Queen driveway. He knew J.T. had slowed up deliberately, allowing him to get to Kayla first. He appreciated it.

Kayla rolled her suitcase out on the huge veranda surrounding the Citrus Queen.

She turned to hug the two friends she'd come to love so fiercely. Arriving back from Marcelo's she'd fallen into their arms and cried her heart out. As usual, they surrounded her with love and good advice. But now she needed space and a place to call her own. She planned to take her time and find a place where she'd never want to leave. That's where she would live the rest of her life. A life without love, void of touch, taste and smell. Without the kisses she craved so badly from her handsome Marcelo.

The ranch felt like home, and she'd never find a place where she'd had so many dreams and plans. Where she'd imagined dark-headed little boys playing happily one minute then rolling each other in the dirt the next.

But no matter where she was physically, spiritually she was closer to God than she'd ever been. Since she'd been with the Fuentes family, they had talked and fellowshipped over God's Word, and when she prayed it was no longer just for her own needs but for those around her, as well. She'd even invited her part-time workers to go to church with her. Whatever else she lost in her life, she would always have the love of her Heavenly Father and right now that was enough.

She drove from the Citrus Queen with a heavy heart but resigned to a future alone. She had one more place to visit before she signed in to a hotel in McAllen.

"Gone?" Marcelo felt ice spreading through his stomach. He sensed rather than saw J.T. come up behind him. "Where'd she go?"

Carina shrugged her shoulders. "She didn't say. Just that she needed to find some place to call home."

For a moment fear, stark and vivid, threatened to overpower him. He felt its closing tentacles about his neck and his breath became shallow, quick gasps. He leaned forward and grabbed his knees, drawing in great gasps of air.

"Marc?" J.T.'s hand clasped his shoulder. Marcelo could hear the worry in his voice.

Fear hath torment. From out of nowhere came the second part of the verse God had used to show him why he'd lost Kayla in the first place. *There is no fear in love; but perfect love casteth out fear: because fear hath torment. He that feareth is not made perfect in love.* How true the Scriptures were because panic and fear gnawed away at his confidence right now, almost crippling him. "Lord, help me." From deep in his soul the words came forth from his mouth. He clenched his jaw to kill the sob in his throat.

Then he felt it, a hand helping him to stand. Yet J.T. had moved to take a weeping Carina in his arms. A newly awakened sense of strength began to gird him with resolve. A cry of relief broke from his lips. At this point he knew he would be okay. God had him in the palm of His hand. He straightened himself with dignity. His future sister-in-law, Carina, flew into his arms, the tears rolling freely down her face. He closed his arms around her but looked over her shoulder into his brother's black eyes. Suspicious moisture glistened in J.T.'s eyes. He lifted his arm and Juan Antonio's arms circled him and Carina. The three of them stood locked together, sorrow heavy on their hearts but Marcelo stepped away and spoke to them with quiet but definite firmness.

"I'm going to find her." When Carina started to speak he held up a hand. "And I will never let her go."

He touched J.T.'s shoulder and ran down the steps. He had no idea where to look but he would not stop till he found her. On the road to Confetti a small voice whispered he was headed the wrong way. Disconcerted, he pulled off the highway and waited a moment for the voice to speak again. And then he knew. He turned the car westward. He was going for his woman.

Kayla watched the dust rise from the vehicle racing down the track and a wave of anticipation swept through her. He'd found her. She had prayed God would send him; had felt in her heart she needed to give it one last try. She had left no clues. No one knew she was here. The door to the line shack was locked so if Marcelo hadn't come this evening she would have taken that as a sign from the Lord to move on. But if it was meant to be, he would find her at the place they first met and fell in love. She'd laid out a fleece of sorts because she was too weak in faith to be more specific in asking the Lord for something so important. If Marcelo seriously sought her with all his heart, he would find her. Well, he'd found her, but would it mean what she wanted it to?

She waited patiently. He pulled the diesel close to the steps. Trying to read the signs, she wondered what that meant. He'd never parked there before. She walked to the edge of the porch and waited for him to come around the front of the truck. He stopped within ten feet of her. His black eyes probed to her very soul but they surveyed her kindly with concern and oh, could it be hope? Longing? She walked down the steps but that's as far as her courage would carry her. Uncertainty chewed her insides. She had touched his arm earlier today and he'd rebuffed her. So she waited.

He took an abrupt step toward her then turned on his heel and strode to the truck. She closed her eyes and covered her face with her hands. Her knees gave out and she sank down on the bottom step. The pain went beyond tears. She heard the truck door close. Then his arms went around her as he knelt in the dust at her feet. "My darling, what's wrong?" The rich timbre of his voice whispered along her sensitive nerves.

"I thought you were leaving." Her fingers explored his face. She touched his lips, his brow. Cupping his face she laid her forehead against his. "I felt adrift, falling, with nothing to hold on to."

Marcelo shushed her, punctuating his words with quick, melting kisses. "My sweet Kayla. Hold on to me because from this day forward I'll never let you go."

"You promise? Even if I do something stupid?"

"We'll both mess up but let's vow right now to talk things out, to yell, stomp, whatever it takes, but let's not do this to each other again. The light went out of my life. I've never been more miserable. I can't bear a life without you in it. *Comprende,* baby?" His kiss was urgent, driven by the vivid recollection of the desolation they'd both experienced.

"Comprendo," she answered softly.

He leaned away and took her hand in his. He slid the diamond ring back on her finger. "This is why I went back to the truck. I never want this returned and

I'll make you a deal right now." He waited expectantly for her agreement, his eyes alive with purpose. She nodded. "You wear this ring and you'll always have a home in my heart."

"Yes." Her voice barely a whisper, she pledged her love to him. He lifted her into his arms and carried her to the truck. "We're going home." Home. An old saying flitted through Kayla's mind. Home is where the heart is. Her heart was with Marcelo.

* * * * *

SPECIAL EXCERPT FROM

Love Inspired

He was her high school crush, and now he's a single father of twins. Allison True just got a second chance at love.

Read on for a sneak preview of
STORYBOOK ROMANCE *by Lissa Manley,*
the exciting fifth book in
THE HEART OF MAIN STREET *series,*
available October 2013.

Something clunked from the back of the bookstore, drawing Allison True's ever-vigilant attention. Her ears perking up, she rounded the end of the front counter. Another clunk sounded, and then another. Allison decided the noise was coming from the Kids' Korner, so she picked up the pace and veered toward the back right part of the store, creasing her brow.

She arrived in the area set up for kids. Her gaze zeroed in on a dark-haired toddler dressed in jeans and a red shirt, slowly yet methodically yanking books off a shelf, one after the other. Each book fell to the floor with a heavy clunk, and in between each sound, the little guy laughed, clearly enjoying the sound of his relatively harmless yet messy play.

Allison rushed over, noting there was no adult in sight. "Hey, there, bud," she said. "Whatcha doing?"

He turned big brown eyes fringed with long, dark eyelashes toward her. He looked vaguely familiar even though she was certain she'd never met this little boy.

"Fun!" A chubby hand sent another book crashing to the floor. He giggled and stomped his feet on the floor in a little happy dance. "See?"

Carefully she reached out and stilled his marauding hands. "Whoa, there, little guy." She gently pulled him away. "The books are supposed to stay on the shelf." Holding on to him, she cast her gaze about the enclosed area set aside for kids, but her view was limited by the tall bookshelves lined up from the edge of the Kids' Korner to the front of the store. "Are you here with your mommy or daddy?"

The boy tugged. "Daddy!" he squealed.

"Nicky!" a deep masculine voice replied behind her. "Oh, man. Looks like you've been making a mess."

A nebulous sense of familiarity swept through her at the sound of that voice. Not breathing, still holding the boy's hand, Allison slowly turned around. Her whole body froze and her heart gave a little spasm then fell to her toes as she looked into deep brown eyes that matched Nicky's.

Sam Franklin. The only man Allison had ever loved.

Pick up STORYBOOK ROMANCE
in October 2013 wherever Love Inspired® Books are sold.

REQUEST YOUR FREE BOOKS!

2 FREE CHRISTIAN NOVELS
PLUS 2
FREE
MYSTERY GIFTS

HEARTSONG
PRESENTS

YES! Please send me 2 Free Heartsong Presents novels and my 2 FREE mystery gifts (gifts are worth about $10). After receiving them, if I don't wish to receive any more books I can return the shipping statement marked "cancel." If I don't cancel, I will receive 4 brand-new novels every month and be billed just $4.24 per book in the U.S. and $5.24 per book in Canada. That's a savings of at least 20% off the cover price. It's quite a bargain! Shipping and handling is just 50¢ per book in the U.S. and 75¢ per book in Canada.* I understand that accepting the 2 free books and gifts places me under no obligation to buy anything. I can always return a shipment and cancel at any time. Even if I never buy another book, the two free books and gifts are mine to keep forever.

159/359 HDN FVYK

Name	(PLEASE PRINT)

Address	Apt. #

City	State	Zip

Signature (if under 18, a parent or guardian must sign)

Mail to the **Harlequin® Reader Service:**
IN U.S.A.: P.O. Box 1867, Buffalo, NY 14240-1867

* Terms and prices subject to change without notice. Prices do not include applicable taxes. Sales tax applicable in N.Y. This offer is limited to one order per household. Not valid for current subscribers to Heartsong Presents books. All orders subject to credit approval. Credit or debit balances in a customer's account(s) may be offset by any other outstanding balance owed by or to the customer. Please allow 4 to 6 weeks for delivery. Offer available while quantities last. Offer valid only in the U.S.

Your Privacy—The Harlequin® Reader Service is committed to protecting your privacy. Our Privacy Policy is available online at www.ReaderService.com or upon request from the Harlequin Reader Service.
We make a portion of our mailing list available to reputable third parties that offer products we believe may interest you. If you prefer that we not exchange your name with third parties, or if you wish to clarify or modify your communication preferences, please visit us at www.ReaderService.com/consumerchoice or write to us at Harlequin Reader Service Preference Service, P.O. Box 9062, Buffalo, NY 14269. Include your complete name and address.

HSPDIR13R

HEARTSONG
PRESENTS

Look out for 4 new
Heartsong Presents books next month!

**Every month 4 inspiring faith-filled
romances will be available in stores.**

These contemporary and historical Christian
romances emphasize God's role in every
relationship and reinforce the importance of
faith, hope and love.

Love Inspired HISTORICAL

Eve Pickering knows what it's like to be judged because of your past. So she's not about to leave the orphaned boy she's befriended alone and unprotected in this unfamiliar Texas town. And if Chance Dawson's offer of shelter is the only way she can look after Leo, Eve will turn it into a warm, welcoming home for the holidays. No matter how temporary it may be—or how much she's really longing to stay for good….

Chance came all the way from the big city to make it on his own in spite of his secret…and his overbearing rich family. But Eve's bravery and caring is giving him a confidence he never expected— and a new direction for his dream. And with a little Christmas luck, he'll dare to win her heart as well as her trust—and make their family one for a lifetime.

Texas Grooms

A Family for Christmas

by

WINNIE GRIGGS

Available October 2013 wherever
Love Inspired Historical books are sold.

LIH82983

Love Inspired.
SUSPENSE
RIVETING INSPIRATIONAL ROMANCE

FALL FROM GRACE by MARTA PERRY

Teacher Sara Esch helps widower Caleb King comfort his daughter who witnessed a crime. But then Sara gets too close to the truth and Caleb must risk it all for the woman who's taught him to love again.

DANGEROUS HOMECOMING by DIANE BURKE

Katie Lapp needs her childhood friend Joshua Miller more than ever when someone threatens her late husband's farm. Katie wants it settled the Amish way...but not everyone can be trusted. Can Joshua protect her...even if it endangers his heart?

RETURN TO WILLOW TRACE by KIT WILKINSON

Lydia Stoltz wants to avoid the man who courted her years ago. But a series of accidents startles their Plain community...and leads her straight to Joseph Yoder. At every turn, it seems their shared past holds the key to their future.

DANGER IN AMISH COUNTRY,
a 3-in-1 anthology including novellas by
MARTA PERRY, DIANE BURKE and
KIT WILKINSON

Available October 2013 wherever
Love Inspired Suspense books are sold.

LIS44558R

Allison True knows that in real life, romances end in heartache.
She learned that the hard way in high school, when handsome
Sam Franklin completely ignored her existence. Back in
Bygones, Allison is older now, and wiser. Her only focus is
keeping her new bookstore afloat, and her heart safe from Sam.

Before he was a single dad juggling rambunctious twins, Sam
had a secret thing for Allison. Now a beautiful young woman
has replaced the bookish girl in braids and glasses, and Sam
must work twice as hard to keep his feelings in check. He
swore off love after his ex shattered his heart and his faith. But
Allison seems to know the secret to repairing both....

The Cowboy's
Christmas Courtship
by Brenda Minton

Available October 2013
wherever Love Inspired books are sold.

LI87843